ERON

STARLIGHT HIGHLANDER MAIL ORDER BRIDES 2

SKYE MACKINNON

Peryton Press

CONTENTS

GLOSSARY

Many of the alien words are taken from Scottish Gaelic (yes, including the flying vagina). Some of them have been slightly changed, while others are exact translations.

Albya – planet of the Albyans (from Alba = Scotland)

Bainnse – wedding

Bawbag – scrotum (Scots insult)

Click – minute (30 Earth minutes are 20 intergalactic clicks)

C-suit – camouflage suit that helps aliens blend in with humans

Fraoch – a shrub plant similar to heather

Lady Beyra – Albyan Goddess (based on the Scottish/Celtic Beira myth)

Leannan – sweetheart, my love

Migges – midges (tiny mosquitos aka miniature demons who love to torment this particular author in her garden)

Pit air iteig – for fuck's sake (literally: flying vagina)

Rotation – Albyan year

Quantnet – intergalactic internet

Sgid/sgidding – fuck/fucking

Taigeis – a fluffy round animal based on the Scottish haggis

Ton air eigh dhut – fuck you (literally: may your arse hit the ice)

Uisge beatha – whisky (literally: water of life)

1

June

Cupid wore a kilt. I blinked at the garish logo of the dating agency, wishing I was somewhere else. If Anna hadn't sat next to me, I'd have left half an hour ago.

"Don't look like you're about to be tortured and burned at the stake," Anna whispered. "This will be fun."

She was my best friend, but sometimes, I wanted to throttle her.

If only I hadn't agreed to that bet. I'd been drunk out of my mind and it had seemed like a good idea at the time. In retrospect, it was clear that Anna had tricked me. She knew I was rubbish at darts. She knew that I couldn't resist a challenge. And she'd made me drunk as a sailor by keeping me supplied with mojitos.

Now I was trapped.

"I'm only going to sign up," I told her firmly. "I won't reply if they find a match."

Anna rolled her eyes. "Haven't you seen their ads? If your match is even half as hot as the guys in the advert, you'll want to meet him."

She was right. The men on the Hot Tatties Dating Agency posters were drool-worthy with their kilts, their muscles, their proud faces. The agency specialised in Scottish men and took full advantage of their clientele's sexiness. Anna's sister-in-law had worked on the agency's marketing and had even found herself a Highlander of her own. I'd never met either of them, but they were the reason why Anna had persuaded me - no, forced me - to come here today.

"I'm happily single," I complained. "Self-partnered. I like having no commitments."

Anna snorted. "And that's why you were lamenting how lonely you were last night."

I couldn't remember saying that, but my head still pounded with a hangover and I only recalled maybe half of what we'd talked about. It was all a bit foggy. I'd not been that drunk in years. My friends were all married or in long-term relationships, some had kids, and none of them wanted to go out partying like we used to.

Maybe Anna was right and it was time to settle down. Find a guy to have more than a one-night-thing with. Buy a house. Get a dog.

No, that wasn't me. I wasn't that kind of woman. I loved my independence. Marriage was for other people.

"June Summer?" The receptionist looked around the waiting room. I'd been surprised that we weren't the only people wanting to register with the agency - but then, their ads were everywhere.

Anna pulled me to my feet and waved at the young woman. "That's us."

"Let go of me," I hissed. She only grinned and tightened her grip on my arm as if she was worried I'd run away. She wasn't wrong.

She forced me to follow the receptionist into a larger office. The dark pink wallpaper was garish and together with the fluffy pink cushions and the red carpet, it made me think of a brothel. Behind a desk sat a woman in her forties, above her another large kilt-wearing cupid.

She got up and walked around the desk to greet us with a handshake. "I'm Pam, owner of Hot Tatties. Thanks for coming."

"Anna," my friend introduced herself. "And this is June. She's the one to register, I'm already happily married."

Pam gave me a wide grin. "You're not the only one to bring a friend. It's always nice to have some support. Take a seat, I'll bring over the tablets. Would you like some tea? Coffee? Hot chocolate?"

I'd planned to say no until she mentioned the chocolate. I could never resist a sweet treat like that. At least that would almost make this experience worth it.

"Hot chocolate, please," I said.

Anna nodded. "Same."

While Pam got our drinks, I stared at the row of picture frames on the wall opposite. Ten men smiled at me, all of them gorgeous, all of them wearing kilts, all of them very lickable. I was starting to think that the agency used models for their marketing, not actual guys. What were the chances of finding ten perfect but *single* men like these? Guys who looked like that weren't single. And they certainly wouldn't choose someone like me.

"We should go," I muttered. "This doesn't feel right."

Anna took my hand, either to reassure me or to keep me in place; I wasn't sure. "We're staying. You lost the bet. You have to do it."

Before I could give her a very angry reply, Pam returned with a tray. She'd added a bowl of shortbread. How very Scottish. I wrapped my hands around my mug to stop myself from fidgeting. I always did that when I was nervous.

Pam put a tablet on the table in front of us. "We've got a questionnaire for you to complete. We can either do it as a sort of interview or you can fill it in yourself, whatever you prefer. Then I'll take a few quick pictures, you spit in a tube and we're done."

Had I heard her right? "Spit in a tube?"

She smiled. "We've got access to the latest DNA matching technology. Scientists have found certain markers that can tell if someone's a good match." She lowered her voice. "I personally like to call it the soulmates test, but that might put off the people who don't believe in fated mates. Do you?"

"Yes," Anna said immediately. "The moment I met Ewan, I knew that we were meant together."

I'd always envied her for that. Ewan and Anna really were perfect for each other. I'd never seen them fight. They fit together like two jigsaw pieces.

"And what about you, June?" Pam asked.

I shrugged. "I guess there may be soulmates for some people, but I don't believe every person has one."

"Well, if your soulmate is in our register, we will find him. Or do you prefer women?"

"No, men are good. I mean, women are nice too, but not for me."

"I understand. You'll be pleased to know that we currently have over eleven thousand men on our roster and that number is rising daily. I wish I had that many women signing up. Don't get me wrong, we have ladies sign up every day, but I lack the manpower to recruit even more. Anyway, that's my problem, not yours. I'm sure we'll find you the perfect match." She picked up the tablet. "Let's do it this way, that's more fun for me."

She gave us a wide grin. Her enthusiasm was strangely infectious. I suddenly didn't feel as negative about it all. Maybe she was right. Maybe my soulmate was out there, waiting for me.

"June Summer, is that right?"

I nodded, waiting for some comment or joke on my name. Everyone did it. But Pam moved on to the next question right away. How refreshing.

"Age?"

"Thirty-two, although my birthday is next month."

"Your birthday is in June? Is that why your parents gave you the name?"

I sighed. "Aye. They were idiots."

"I think it's kind of sweet," Pamela said while typing. "Where do you currently live? And would you be willing to relocate?"

"I'm in Dumbarton, but I work here in Glasgow. And I suppose... for the right person, I could potentially move, yes."

Not that I expected this to happen, but if I had to be here, why not indulge Pam.

"Good. Most of our men prefer the ladies to move in with them rather than the other way round. They live in a beautiful place, though. If I wasn't married already, I'd grab myself one of them." She winked and I couldn't help but return her smile.

"They all live in one place?" I asked.

"Mostly. It's a large area though, so don't worry, you'll have privacy. They're split into clans who each have their own towns."

"Wait, towns? I thought they lived in the Highlands. There aren't many towns there. I think I'd know if there were towns full of sexy, I mean, good-looking guys walking around in kilts. Everyone would flock there."

Pam smirked. "They don't like prospective matches know too much about where they're located, exactly because of that. They want and need to be selective about their partners which is why everything is handled through Hot Tatties. But let's move on. What do you do for a living?"

I hated that question because the answer made me sound like the most boring woman ever. "I work in finance."

"Oh, I'd never have guessed that. Lovely. What do you like to do in your free time?"

On and on the questions went until Pam finally put the tablet down. My mug had been empty for at least ten minutes and I was ready to leave.

"That was fun," Anna whispered while the agency owner rummaged around her desk. "I didn't know you liked clay-pigeon shooting and hill walking."

I made sure Pam wasn't listening before I replied. "I made that up to make me sound more interesting. My hobbies are so boring. Besides, it's not like anyone will ever find out that I lied."

She gave me a doubtful look but didn't say anything.

Pam waved a camera, beckoning me to get up. "Stand in front of that wall over there, dear. This is mostly for my own purposes. It always helps me remember the ladies I've met while I search for a match."

"Does that mean nobody else will get to see the picture?"

"Only if you're matched and give permission to have me pass on your details. We like the women to be in control of the process."

I liked that. I smiled for the camera, feeling a little self-conscious. I was wearing my business suit since Anna had picked me up at my office. Not what I'd wear for a first date. But this wasn't real, I reminded myself. Just to placate my friend after losing a bet.

Happy with the photos she'd taken, Pam handed me a plastic vial. "Now I just need your sample and then we're all done for the day."

I gave the vial a doubtful look. Spitting into it in front of them seemed embarrassing, although I wasn't quite sure why. People spat on the pavements all the time without thinking. I sighed and did as she'd asked. Pam screwed the vial shut and put it in a plastic bag decorated with the kilted cupid logo. That little half-naked creature really was everywhere.

"I'll be in touch once I find a match," Pam chirped. "I'm sending the next batch of samples to the lab tonight, so it might be sooner than you think."

No, it wouldn't be. I wasn't going to get a match and even if I did, I wasn't going to meet them.

This wasn't real. It was just to make Anna happy. I was going to stay single.

2

Eron

I picked up the baby taigeis and tickled its fluffy belly.

"I'm sorry, wee one," I whispered, very aware of the animal's sensitive hearing. "You're going to have to stay with me now."

I carried him out of the nursery, where his mother lay dead on the floor. I was going to examine her body later to find out how she'd died. For now, I had to keep the little cub separate from the others in case he had the same virus his mother had died from. He wasn't the first taigeis I'd hand-raised and he wouldn't be the last.

He looked up at me with big eyes, his massive black pupils almost drowning out the dark brown surrounding them. He was a purebred Highland taigeis and worth my attention. He'd fetch a fair price once he was fully grown. I never had the heart to send the hand-raised taigeis to the butcher. They either became part of my breeding programme or were sold as pets.

Before I'd started my farm, having a taigeis as a pet was unheard of. It was thought they were impossible to tame. Now, people thought it was easy, having read about me. It wasn't. Even after many rotations of tending to my taigeis, I still learned new things all the time. If I didn't have a medpod stashed away in my basement, I would have been covered in scars by now. Taigeis were small but vicious. Even the ones who'd lived on my farm for rotations could be unpredictable. This little cub was cute and fluffy now, but once it was fully grown, its teeth would be sharp and lethal. It was a joke of evolution to produce an animal so cute that it made even the most hardened warrior want to cuddle it, while at the same time giving it the temper of a predator.

The little taigeis curled up in my arms, its eyes falling shut. A moment later, he was fast asleep. His little nose twitched as we walked through the cool morning air. It was going to be a beautiful day. The sun painted the mountains in the distance a burnt orange, turning the landscape into a painting. My sister would have loved to paint the sunrise. She'd always loved the countryside, unlike me, who'd preferred living in the centre of Priomh, the Albyan capital. It was a melting pot where all the clans came together. I'd enjoyed the noise, the smells, the constant new experiences. My past self would be aghast at seeing me live in the middle of nowhere, surrounded only by animals.

It had taken time for me to come to appreciate the desolate beauty of the mountains the taigeis were native to. Their steep slopes were covered in fraoch, a spikey plant with tiny purple flowers that painted the hills a bright colour every heat season. The first purple dots were visible even from here and it wouldn't be long until the entire slopes had changed colour. It was my favourite time of the year.

I made a mental note to drive to the mountains tomorrow to get some shrubs for the taigeis. They loved nibbling on the branches, miraculously able to avoid the thorns. But first, I had to get the little cub settled.

It was pleasantly cool inside my farmhouse. The smell of fresh bread made me smile. For once, I'd remembered to programme my food processor in advance so I'd have a warm loaf for my morning meal. The cub's nose twitched again.

"That's not for you, little one," I muttered, stroking its furry head. "I have different food for you."

I got a bottle of taigeis milk from the cooler. One of my best-kept secrets. I'd found a way to milk two of the tame taigeis females. They didn't enjoy it, but it was the best way of keeping any motherless cub alive. I'd experimented with substitute milk, but it wasn't as good as the real thing. The scratches were worth it if it meant saving a cub's life.

"Time to wake up." I nudged the little furball. As soon as the nozzle touched his lips, he began to suck greedily. He didn't even open his eyes. For him, life was simple. Eat, drink, sleep, and once he was fully grown, mate and produce offspring. He knew nothing of the troubles we Albyans faced. I was almost jealous.

The cub burped before settling back to sleep. I chuckled and carried him over to the room I'd dubbed the nursery. I couldn't remember how many cubs I'd hand-reared in here, getting up throughout the night to feed them. Ten, maybe? More? I'd have to check my notes so I'd know what to call this one. I never gave them names. I didn't want to grow attached.

I gently lay him into the artificial burrow I'd created out of a box and some cloth. I'd check on him once I'd cleaned out the stables. But first, the morning meal. The bread should be ready by now.

A beep somewhere in the house made me sigh. Where had I left my commstick this time? I kept losing the sgidding thing. Back in Priomh, I would have asked the inbuilt AI to search for it, but I didn't have such technology in my farmhouse. I'd thought I'd miss it, but I didn't.

By the time I finally found the commstick in a boot in the hallway, it had stopped ringing. No idea how it had got there. Some days I could swear it had legs to run and hide when I wasn't looking. I had several missed calls from Cyle. I sighed. He just wouldn't give up.

While I scrolled through the notifications, a new message popped up.

Call me. It's urgent.

My curiosity piqued, I dialled his number, making sure the holo function was turned off. I wasn't in the mood to see people, even if it was my friend.

He answered immediately. "How are you, my favourite hermit?"

"Busy. What's so urgent?"

"You've been matched."

"Huh?"

Cyle groaned. "Please tell me you've been reading my messages? Watched the news?"

"Been busy."

"Turn on your holo. I want to see your face when I tell you."

I was tempted to hang up on him. Why was he my friend again?

"Just tell me what's going on," I growled. "I'm hungry and you know what that means."

"I remember from our days at the Academy." Cyle laughed. "I'm glad we're not in the same room just now."

"Tell. Me."

"I found a planet full of compatible females," he said before leaving a dramatic pause. I tried to process his words. Compatible females.

"You mean... mates?"

"Indeed. And one region of this planet is culturally very similar to Albya. My brother already found his mate among the females there. How did you not see this on the news? On the quantnet? It was everywhere."

"I've been busy," I said for the third time. "The taigeis don't feed themselves."

"Indeed. And one region of this planet is culturally very similar to Albya. My brother already found his mate among the females there. How did you not see this on the news? On the quantnet? It was everywhere."

"I've been busy," I said for the third time. "The taigeis don't feed themselves."

"There's more to life than your animals, my dear friend. When did you last venture outside your farm? How about you come to Priomh and I'll tell you everything that happened?"

"I have a motherless cub to take care of, one of my bulls has to be isolated because he's too aggressive, and the price of their supplement fodder has gone up. Again. I have bigger worries, Cyle."

"Bigger worries than finding a mate?" he asked dubiously. "I'm not sure you understand what this means. We're no longer going extinct! That's more important than an aggressive taigeis. I'm hopeful that we might be able to use the Peritans to find a cure to the Sleep. It might not be long until we can wake our females - including your sister."

I staggered backwards until my back hit the wall. Waking my sister. Curing her from the Sleep. I'd long since given up hope to ever talk to her again. Ever hear her beautiful voice again. That's what I missed most of all. She'd been a singer at the Albyan Arthouse in Priomh, delighting audiences every night. She'd succumbed to the Sleep on stage, collapsing before I could reach her.

"How can they help you find a cure?" I asked when I'd regained control.

"I don't know yet, but I have a good feeling. My brother's mate has agreed to take part in my research. We started with establishing the link between her and Thorrn. I've managed to identify the marker in their genetic code that's responsible for the mating bond. Our partners on Peritus have been busy gathering samples from willing females - and one of them is your match."

I wasn't a male who was often lost for words. I didn't speak much, but when I did, I always knew what to say. In this moment, I had no idea how to respond.

A match. I had a mate. An alien mate. A female meant to be mine. I'd given up hope of ever finding a mate. With all Albyan females either asleep or dead, all of us males had come to the sad realisation that we were doomed to stay alone. I'd resigned myself to tending to my taigeis for the rest of my life. Maybe hire an assistant once I grew too old to keep the farm running by myself. But I'd planned to wait with that until I had no other choice. Albyan males were naturally dominant and didn't do well living together.

"Are you still there?" Cyle asked.

"Aye. It's... are you sure? How can you be sure I've got a mate? How did you even get my genetic code?"

"Remember when you and Thorrn got yourselves arrested? You were still in the database. We're starting a planet-wide testing scheme but first combined all available datasets, including that of the enforcers."

"And I have a mate?"

"Have the taigeis eaten your brain? Yes, you have! I don't know much about her, but she's on a ship bound for Albyan as we speak. We haven't quite established what we will do once they arrive. Some of my colleagues want to do the first meeting in controlled laboratory conditions, but I'm thinking it will be less stressful for the females to meet their new mates at their homes. It'll give them an insight into how their males live."

"Does that mean you want to bring her here? To my farm?"

I ran a hand over my antennae which were starting to itch. Strange, that had never happened before. Maybe some migges had found their way into the house and stung me.

"I'll let you know as soon as we've decided. But between us, you might want to get your guest room ready."

3

June

They didn't give me any warning. The red letter on my desk came as a shock. I was fired. Well, technically, they offered me an ad-hoc consultant role to be called upon whenever they had a need. No, thanks. I'd given this company everything and what did I get in return? Nothing.

At least they didn't insist on me working the four weeks to my official leaving date and put me on paid leave instead. I bet my bosses thought themselves charitable doing so. Fucking bawbags. I didn't swear a lot, but this was one of the few occasions where I wished I had a more extensive expletive vocabulary. Bloody cunts. Fuckers. Sheepshaggers.

I spent the afternoon and evening in various bars, drinking away my anger. I'd never been fired before.

Until now, it had always been me who'd handed in my notice. They'd not even given me a proper reason, just that they had to cut costs. I shouldn't be surprised that it was me they'd let go and not one of my male colleagues. I'd heard it too many times: customers preferred talking to a man about their finances. Males were seen as more knowledgeable when it came to money.

Idiots.

I was the most qualified in my department, yet here I was, jobless, drunk and furious. I'd show them. I'd find a new job, better paid, where they valued my skills and experience. This wasn't the only company in town. But first, I deserved a holiday. Yes. That would be nice. I'd done way too much overtime in the past few years, only taking days off for Christmas and to visit my parents in the summer. They lived in Spain, preferring the warmth over Scotland's dreich weather, but we weren't close enough for me to visit them more often. Once a year was enough for my mother to tell me that she wanted grandchildren, preferably right now.

I fell asleep on the train, almost missing my stop, and by the time I finally got to my flat, I was close to keeling over. I staggered inside and almost slipped on a large envelope. The cupid logo on the back of it made me rip it open. It had been two weeks since Anna had dragged me to the dating agency. I'd not heard anything since and almost forgotten about it.

I let myself fall onto the sofa and read the letter at the very top of a stack of papers. My vision was blurry and it took me forever to decipher the small writing.

Dear Miss Summer,

We're pleased to tell you that we've found a match for you!

Thanks to our state-of-the-art genetic matching technology, we are 100% certain that he is the perfect match. We are so sure of the accuracy of your match that we'd like to offer you an all-expenses-paid trip to meet your match. You can find more information about this in the attached documents.*

We are still waiting to hear back from our partner agency, so at the moment, we don't have a lot of information on your match yet. However, we've enclosed a photograph along with all other details we've been given.

Also attached are login details for our member portal where you'll be able to confirm your attendance on this once-in-a-lifetime trip to your match's location.

We're hoping to hear from you soon.

Best wishes,

Hot Tatties Dating Agency

** We don't like to use the term 'soul mate', but that's exactly what he is!*

I re-read the letter twice just to make sure my drunken brain was processing it correctly. Hadn't I just decided that I needed a holiday? And here they were, offering me one. The bit about meeting some guy was secondary.

I rummaged through the documents in the envelope until I found a glossy brochure. First-class travel. Free food including local delicacies. Hotel accommodation. Various sightseeing trips. They even included a stipend to visit local retailers. Seriously? This had to be fake. Why would a dating agency pay me to go shopping?

Maybe it was a cooperation with some tourism programme. Supporting local retailers, local restaurants and all that. Or maybe I was too drunk to realise why it made sense.

If I'd received this letter without having been at the agency in person, I would have thrown it in the bin. But I'd met Pam and she'd seemed genuine. There was no mention of me having to pay any money myself. What was the harm in signing up? I could really do with a holiday.

On the back of the brochure, it gave two dates to choose from. The first was two days from now. And wait, that couldn't be right. Three months? That had to be a mistake. That was more than just a holiday.

Three months. A quarter of a year. Crazy. I supposed they really wanted us to get to know our matches. Would it be so bad to be away for that long? I no longer had a job. Yes, I'd have to keep paying rent for my flat, but I wouldn't have any other living costs, so it was actually cheaper than staying here. Maybe a bit of money for souvenirs, but it sounded like the agency would pay for everything. It sounded too good to be true. And I was totally going to sign up for it.

I reached for my laptop and logged into the Hot Tatties portal. The most beautiful man I'd ever seen popped up on the screen. Dark blue eyes the colour of the sea on a stormy day. Shoulder-length ginger hair that framed his angular face. A rugged beard that made me want to run my fingers along his jaw. And he wore a kilt. Nothing other than a kilt, the same deep indigo as his eyes. His muscular chest was covered in hair that somehow made him appear even more masculine, if that was even possible. Usually, I didn't like hairy chests, but with him, it was different. On his right shoulder was a Celtic tattoo, some sort of knot design that seemed familiar. It made him even more stereotypically Scottish. I could see him toss cabers with those massive arms. I bet he could play the bagpipes. My eyes flicked to his kilt again and I tried hard not to imagine what pipe he might be hiding under there.

I forced myself to scroll down. Eron of Clan Monadh. 35 years old. Business owner. Lives in Fàsail.

That had to be my match. I quickly checked the envelope and yes, there it was, the same picture. Eron. What an unusual name. I said it a few times. Beautiful. Unless I was pronouncing it the wrong way.

Business owner sounded good. He didn't have annoying bosses who could fire him without warning. I had no idea where Fàsail was, but it sounded Gaelic. Probably some little place deep within the Highlands.

Under the image was lots of text, some kind of contract. Then a field to enter my name and a tick box.

I should think about this. I should wait until I'm sober. I shouldn't do this in my current drunken, depressed, angry state.

I ticked the box, typed my name, smiled at Eron and closed the laptop.

Anna accompanied me to the airport. I had two heavy suitcases with me, but even so, I wasn't sure if it would be enough for three months.

Yesterday, I'd had a long call with Pam who'd reassured me that I'd be provided with everything I'd need, including clothes if I ended up not taking enough. I still couldn't believe that this was real. Things like this didn't happen to me. I'd never won anything in my life. My friends knew me for being perpetually unlucky. Yet here I was, about to go on the holiday of a lifetime.

Meeting Eron was a pleasant but secondary part of it.

"You ready?" Anna asked. She was bouncing with excitement. She'd repeated at least four times how she wished she could come with me. She and Ewan were planning to visit his sister soon, but they hadn't managed to decide on a date yet. As a surgeon, Anna found it hard to take time off. The hospital's administrators were experts at manipulating her to cut holidays short or not take them in the first place.

"I think so."

"Getting last-minute doubts?"

She knew me so well.

Anna wrapped her arms around me and pulled me into one of her legendary hugs. "It'll be fine. You'll love it there. Jenny keeps sending me the most amazing pictures. You'll meet her there for an orientation session."

"I thought she did marketing for the agency?"

Anna laughed. "Her role has changed a little since she fell in love with Thorrn. They're such a cute couple. Anyway, you better go to the gate. Wouldn't want you to miss your flight. I hope it'll pass quickly."

That was another thing we hadn't been told. I had no idea where we were flying or how long the flight would take. But it was too late now to pester Pam with questions. I'd tried that yesterday, but she'd been surprisingly tight-lipped. What she had told me, however, was that I should have read the contract.

I couldn't back out. If I did, I'd have to pay for the flight and any fees incurred. From the way Pam had spoken, I assumed it was a lot of money. And I didn't have that, not now that I'd lost my job. I was in it for better or worse. Three months was doable, even if it turned out to be the worst holiday I'd ever been on.

I took a deep breath and hugged Anna one last time before heading to the gate on my ticket. It didn't state an airline on it, but Pam had made it sound like we were taking a private plane. I'd never flown anything other than economy class, so this was exciting.

At the gate, Pam's assistant stood with a Hot Tatties sign along with nine other women. I gave them a small smile.

"June, just in time," the assistant said cheerily. I'd never caught her name. "Now that we're all here, follow me. Put your luggage into this cart. It'll be taken on board for you. You can put your passports away, you won't need them. We've got a special arrangement with the airport."

Some of the women started whispering, but I kept to myself as we followed the young woman through the airport and through a door with a no entry sign. At the end of a corridor, glass doors slid open and we stepped into the rain. Scotland was saying goodbye with the most typical weather it could conjure.

We were herded into an airport bus which drove us to the very edge of the airport where smaller private planes were parked. None of them looked big enough to accommodate all ten of us.

The bus stopped at a metal gate. Beyond it was nothing but fields. Was the assistant playing a practical joke on us?

"How weird," the woman next to me muttered. She had a beautiful tribal scarf wrapped around her head, a colourful contrast to her elegant black dress. She was the only Black woman in our group. Several scars lined her face, one of them cutting across her right eye, and the side of her neck looked like it had been burnt. But the scars didn't make her any less stunning. I felt inadequate next to her. I was so plain in comparison.

She held out her hand. "I'm Beth."

"June."

"Time to get off the bus," the assistant shouted from the front before I could say anything else.

I exchanged a look with Beth, shrugged, then followed the other women outside. This had to be a joke. There was nothing here but the fence. The closest private plane was a few hundred yards away. We weren't even anywhere near a runway.

"What's going on?" one of the women demanded.

The assistant smiled. "All will be revealed. Literally. Come on, they're waiting for us."

"I don't like this," Beth whispered.

"Do you think they're going to do something to us?" I asked just as quietly, my mind suddenly turning into a cesspit of suspicions. Maybe they were going to traffic us. Or kill us all. Sell our organs. What if there were no matches?

A Highlander appeared on the other side of the gate, grinning widely and waving at us. He hadn't been there a second ago. What the ever-loving Fibonacci sequence?

"Greetings, Steff," the bulky male said, smiling at the assistant. "Is everybody here?"

His accent sounded as if he came from the Western Isles, but it had a strange edge to it that made me think he'd not always lived there. Although if he was one of the foreigners the agency worked with, he wasn't from Scotland at all.

"Yes, all ten ladies. Their luggage should be here any moment." She turned to us. "This is where I leave you. Mack will take great care of you."

The thought of her leaving us made me even more anxious. She was our only link to the agency, to the people who knew where we were. What would Anna and Ewan do if they didn't hear from me within a few weeks? Would they go to the police or simply assume that I was having too much fun to call them? And even if they did notify the police, what could they do? By then, we might all be dead.

I hugged my arms around my chest. This was the last chance to run.

"I know this all seems strange, but give it a few more minutes and everything will make sense," Steff said. "Please, follow Mack."

She unlocked the gate and stepped aside.

Last chance.

Next to me, Beth sighed. "I've got nowhere else to go," she muttered to herself and walked through the gate.

Mack grinned at her. "I'll make sure you get the best room."

For some reason, that spurned on everyone else and a moment later, I was the last one on this side of the fence.

Steff put a hand on my shoulder. "It'll be alright, June. You'll see."

"Will I?"

She smiled. "Let's say it this way. If I had a match among the Albyans, not a thousand horses could hold me back. You're so lucky to have been matched. Don't throw away this opportunity." She lowered your voice. "If you talk to Mack... could you ask him to take the test? I feel like he might be my, you know, my match."

Her cheeks turned pink and that's what made me decide to trust her. I couldn't imagine that this young, infatuated woman had any sinister plans.

"I will," I promised and joined the others.

Steff closed the gate behind us. "Safe travels!"

"Silly female," Mack grumbled as he led us along a dirt path. "The Starlight is the best ship in the galaxy. There's no question about safety."

I was still processing his words when the air suddenly shimmered and a UFO appeared in front of us. Gasps filled the air, but I was too shocked to make a sound. If I hadn't heard the other women exclaim in surprise, I would have thought I was hallucinating.

It was a flying saucer like in the movies. Round, silver, as big as a football field. Two kilted men stood by a ramp, waving at us.

"Come aboard, lassies," Mack said cheerfully, seemingly clueless that this wasn't supposed to be happening. Aliens didn't exist. Spaceships were the stuff of films and books. We had sent rockets into space, we had a space station and satellites, but we didn't have flying saucers.

At least there were no little green men. Mack and the other two men looked entirely human. Yes, they were a little taller than average, but not enough to look twice. If they weren't aliens, did that mean they were time travellers? Humans from the future? Somehow, that thought was less unsettling than aliens.

I slowly followed Mack, my legs sluggish and my mind whirling. This wasn't real. I had to be dreaming.

Our group grew quiet when we reached the ramp. One of the males stepped forward, his grin fading into a more serious expression.

"Welcome to the Starlight. I'm Captain Ghorr and I'm honoured to welcome you on board. This is a historic moment. You don't know how pleased we all are to have found you."

The man next to him nodded solemnly. "We're so honoured. We will do everything we can to make this journey as comfortable and enjoyable as possible.

You've each been assigned a suite and your bags will be brought there shortly. As First Officer, I'm responsible for your wellbeing, so please let me know whenever you need something or have concerns."

"Thank you, Kitar," the Captain said. "We will show you your suites later, but for take-off, I'm going to ask you to follow me to the passenger lounge where you can strap in. Your planet's atmosphere sometimes makes take off a little bumpy."

I could only gape at them. Your planet. Not his. Not theirs. Aliens.

This would have been the perfect moment to faint. One of the women behind me did so, collapsing into Mack's arms. He lifted her as if she wore nothing and carried her into the ship. As one, we followed, driven by some herd instinct that made us stick together.

As soon as we'd crossed the ramp, the metal floor beneath my feet started moving, like one of those moving walkways at airports. It carried us into the belly of the ship while behind us, the ramp was pulled in and doors shut out the daylight.

We were trapped on a spaceship.

4

Eron

Priomh felt bigger than I remembered. People kept bumping into me as I made my way to Thorrn's home. Since I'd moved away, they'd named the capital a congestion-free zone, meaning I'd had to park my shuttle in one of the dedicated spots outside the city centre. I could have taken one of the hover buses, but I didn't feel like being surrounded by other males in a small space.

The air here was nothing like the crisp, fresh air I was used to. I missed home already. What a hermit I'd become. My cousin had agreed to look after the taigeis while I was away, but I couldn't wait to get back to my animals. He may have been a vet, but he had only limited experience with taigeis from the few times I'd called him for emergencies. I could deal with minor injuries and illnesses myself, but from time to time, a taigeis got itself into trouble or into a fight and I needed the expertise of a real vet.

Thorrn's house was enormous. I hadn't realised just how rich his fights had made him. It was ridiculous that he got paid for smashing in other males' skulls. I'd not spoken to him beyond telling him my arrival date, so I didn't know if he'd continue his gladiator life or if he'd retire now that he had a mate. I was excited to meet her. She was the same species as my supposed mate. Peritan from a backwater planet called Peritus. I'd never heard of it, which made sense because it hadn't developed space travel yet. The Albyan Elders had had to convince the Intergalactic Council that Peritans were vital to our survival. Cyle and his team had been granted permission for mates to be taken from Peritus and sent to Albya, but only a handful of natives knew about us.

I held my commstick against the white door and it opened silently. White was such an impractical colour. Back home, it would be covered in taigeis shit within days.

"We're upstairs," Thorrn's loud voice sounded as soon as I stepped through the door. "And take off your shoes!"

I chuckled. He'd been domesticated.

Thorrn greeted me at the top of the stairs. He was wearing a stained apron that had seen better days.

"She's teaching me to cook," he said proudly. "The midday meal will be ready shortly. Do you want something to drink?"

"I wouldn't say no to some uisge beatha, if you have some of that 14-year-old left."

Thorrn grinned. "I always have a bottle of that stashed at the back of the cabinet. For special visitors only. Come, make yourself at home. My mate says she needs to stay with the pot or our food will burn."

"Burn? Are you sure having her cook is a good idea?"

He shrugged. "I have a fire alarm. Now take a seat and I'll get you that dram."

His living area had changed since I'd last visited. Utilitarian furniture had given way to comfortable and colourful fittings. Lots of fabric and fluffy pillows. Random ornaments on shelves that served no purpose. Thorrn was no longer the bachelor I'd once known. Would I have to change my own house once my mate arrived?

I left my bags by the door and chose the largest chair. It was a habit of mine. I'd always been a big male, but working on a farm had made me even bulkier. I was lucky Albyans didn't wear shirts. I would have hated to squeeze my arms into fabric confines.

The chair's nano fibres automatically moulded around my body, giving me support from all sides. I didn't have such fancy furniture back home. Would the female expect it? Would she be appalled at my rustic house? Maybe I should go shopping before she arrived. It wasn't that I lacked the credits. I just hadn't thought of improving my home before.

Thorrn returned and handed me a drink. I gave it a swirl, nodding appreciatively when the golden liquid left an oily trace on the inside of the glass. It was a sign of quality.

"To females," my friend said and lifted his glass.

"To females." I took a big sip and shuddered when the uisge beatha burned down my throat. My tongue tingled as pain gave way to flavour.

"This is a good one," I said before emptying my glass. "You should give me a bottle to take home."

"I should? How about you buy your own? I've heard you make quite a nice profit with your taigeis."

"Darling, stop encouraging the stereotype of the stingy Scot!" a female voice called.

Thorrn rolled his eyes. "She thinks we're Scottish. That's where she's from, a country called Scotland. The men there also wear kilts. It's why we're so compatible with their females."

"Our kilts make us compatible?" I asked.

"Maybe, maybe not. My brother will have answers for us soon. We had another session earlier today. I'm not sure why my mate still has to attend them even though they've prodded every bit of her. They've scanned her so often that they must have enough data. But it's in the contract." He sighed.

"What contract?"

"Do you ever watch the news?"

I shrugged. "I sometimes watch animal programmes. They don't talk about the latest husbandry techniques in the news, so it's irrelevant."

"One day, you're going to have to return to society. You can't hide out there forever."

"Yes, I can. Besides, I leave the farm once a week to visit my sister."

"Who's in a facility twenty clicks from you. That doesn't count."

I wished I could tell him why I'd moved away from everyone. Why I kept to myself. Why having strangers on my farm - even a female who may be my mate - was dangerous.

"Thorrn, can you help me?" his female shouted.

My friend shot to his feet and was out of the room in an instant. I chuckled to myself. She had him firmly in her grip. If he wasn't careful, he'd become too tame. Part of being a fighter was presenting a rough exterior to the world. Showing emotion would make him appear weak.

He returned carrying a large tray full of steaming bowls. Behind him, a red-haired female entered the room wearing a traditional Albyan dress. She put her own tray on the table before hurrying over to me. She held out a hand.

"You need to shake it," Thorrn called from across the room. "It's their way of saying hello."

I grasped her hand with two of mine and shook it with enthusiasm.

The female winced. "Hi. Next time, a little less pressure."

Thorrn was by her side immediately. "Did he hurt you?" He glared at me. I had no doubt that he'd attack me if she said yes.

"Don't worry, it's fine. But I shall add this to my list of things we need to teach the males."

"'Teach?" I repeated.

"I'm setting up a syllabus for introductory sessions," the female explained. "One for the women, one for the Albyan males. Thorrn and I have experience in just how different our cultures are."

Thorrn chuckled. "I still can't believe you wear clothes when you go swimming. It's so unnecessary."

"You need to keep your clothes on in public," she said in a tone that made it obvious this wasn't the first time they'd had that conversation.

He gave her an indulgent look before turning to me. "Eron, this is my mate, Jenny. Jenny, this is my oldest friend, Eron."

"Pleasure to meet you," she said with a warm smile. If my mate was only half as friendly and pretty as her, I'd be a happy male.

"Yes," I said before realising that wasn't the correct response. "It's nice to meet you, too."

Jenny chuckled. "Now I know why he's your friend. You both have your foot in your mouth."

I exchanged a confused look with Thorrn. I was glad it was he who asked, "What do you mean? My feet are on the floor. So are Eron's. Do you want us to conduct some sort of acrobatics?"

The female started laughing. "Yet another expression to add to my *idioms for idiots* list. It's becoming quite a long one."

"Peritans have peculiar phrases," Thorrn whispered to me. "Sometimes I think the BrainTrain didn't work correctly, but it must be just their strange way of talking. Some of their expressions make no sense at all.

Wait until your mate tells you to drop it. Don't actually drop what you're holding."

"It was such a lovely vase," Jenny sighed. "But anyway, the food's getting cold."

I was used to eating in silence. Jenny and Thorrn were not. They made me answer their questions even though I wanted to focus on the delicious food. They'd created a blend of Albyan and Peritan cuisine, with some dishes very recognisable while others were alien. I took seconds and then thirds until I couldn't eat a single more bite.

"Glad you liked it," Thorrn said drily. "Maybe don't eat like that in front of your mate. She'll think you're a glutton."

"And what if I am? I'm not going to change my ways. No chance." My mood soured. As much as I was getting used to the idea of having my own female, I wouldn't - and couldn't - change my life for her. It was too dangerous. Maybe I should go back home. It had been a bad idea to even come to Priomh. All for a theory. It wasn't even clear if I really had a match. We wouldn't know until I faced the female. Only if my antennae activated would I know the truth.

I wasn't sure if I could get through the disappointment if she wasn't my mate.

"What's wrong?" Jenny asked. "You suddenly look sad."

"Nothing. I should go."

"Go?" Thorrn boomed. "Home? I don't think so, friend. Even if I have to drag you to the spaceport myself. You have a mate. Half the planet is jealous of you. Don't throw this opportunity away just because you don't like people."

"I like people. Just not..." I shook my head. It was no use. I couldn't explain my reasons without telling them my secret. "When do they arrive?"

Thorrn pulled out his commstick. "They're already in orbit, so it won't be long. We should head to the spaceport. Jenny is going to give a quick introductory talk to you and the other males there before you get to meet the Peritans. They'll sleep in a hotel here in Priomh so they can get adjusted to the atmosphere and gravity. Tomorrow you can take her home."

Take her home. I wasn't prepared at all. Everything was going so fast. I'd meet my mate today. If she was indeed my mate. A shiver ran down my back.

My life was about to change forever.

5

June

It was strange how fast we all got used to being on a spaceship. After the initial shock, it really started to feel like a holiday. The alien men on board did everything they could to make us happy. No request was too big. They vied for our attention and tried to outdo each other constantly. It was kind of adorable. I'd heard Captain Ghorr admonish some of the crew for getting too close to some of the women. It made me feel surprisingly safe. There wasn't a single female alien. Initially, it had been intimidating to be surrounded by nothing but massive half-naked guys who towered above us. Especially once they'd taken off their camouflage suits to reveal that they had four arms. They'd worn them for the first two days to make us feel at ease, but they'd been visibly happier once they'd been able to get rid of them.

Besides the four arms, they also had antennae growing from their foreheads, pink and thin with a round tip. Kitar had explained that they helped Albyan males find their mates. During the first few days on the Starlight, the men had taken turns meeting every female, pushing their antennae towards us as if they were hoping the matching process had been wrong. None of them were successful and once they realised, they stopped invading our personal space.

The ship was big enough to give us some privacy if we wanted to be on our own. I spent a lot of time on the running track that circled the main passenger lounge. The walls could be programmed to show various sceneries, so I'd run on the bottom of the ocean, in the rainforest and in an alien desert with bright blue sand. Running was my way of coping.

In the evenings, we got together to watch films, both Earth classics and Albyan movies. It was a good chance of testing our language skills. We'd each been given BrainTrain earplugs that we had to wear at night. I didn't quite understand how they worked, but after three nights, I could talk Albyan Prime more or less fluently. Kitar, the First Officer, had then programmed other languages into our earplugs depending on where on Albya our mates were from.

I'd asked Kitar if he could get the BrainTrain plugs to teach us other Earth languages. I'd always wanted to learn Italian. He'd declined, but said that on Albya, my mate would be able to purchase language upgrades if I still wanted to do so. I'd ignored his comment about there being no need for speaking Earth languages since I wouldn't return there anyway.

There were three distinct groups among us women. The ones who couldn't wait to meet their mates and become citizens of Albya. The ones who felt deceived and wanted to return home as soon as possible. And then there was the third group, myself included, who weren't quite sure what to think.

Even now, after four weeks with plenty of time to ponder my situation, I still didn't know what I felt. On the one hand, this was one big, amazing adventure. Not many people had ever left our planet. We were pioneers. It was exciting. We were making history. Not something I'd ever thought myself doing. I was a financial advisor. I wasn't anything special. I'd never expected nor wanted to change the world with my job. Now I was on the way to an alien planet.

At the same time, I felt like Pam and the agency had betrayed my trust. They'd never mentioned that the hot Highlanders were aliens. I'd signed up without having all the information. Yes, I'd been drunk and hadn't read the fine print, but even so, it didn't seem right. It may not have been an alien abduction with bright lights and mooing cows, but I wasn't here entirely voluntarily either. I'd expected a holiday on *Earth*.

Granted, neither in the info brochure nor in the contract did it state the *planet* of where our mates were based. I'd checked multiple times. For my mate, it simply said Fàsail as his location. We wouldn't be able to sue Hot Tatties. Not that it would do us any good if we were stranded on the other side of the galaxy.

The Captain had shown us a map of our route, explaining that if humans tried to make this journey with our current technology, it would take about two hundred years to reach Albya. We'd done the trip in one month. Now it made sense why we'd agreed to be away for three months. One month to get there, one month on the planet, one month to get back home - if we wanted to. Some of the women had already said that if they liked their match, they'd stay. Beth was one of them. She'd not said much about her life on Earth, but it was clear she'd not been happy. I assumed it had something to do with her scars.

"Please take your seats in the passenger lounge," Captain's Ghorr's voice came through the tannoy. "We're now in orbit around Albya and will be landing shortly. Don't worry about your belongings. They will be brought to your lodgings."

My heart started beating faster. We were about to land. The four weeks really had passed in a flash. Spa treatments, amazing food, crafting workshops, gym training, lots and lots of cocktails, endless hours of reading in the observatory where I could watch the stars...it had felt a bit like a cruise. I'd never been this relaxed in my life. No stressful job, just free time to do with as I wished. I did miss fresh air, though. We'd been reassured that the atmosphere on Albya was breathable for us, so I couldn't wait to breathe something that didn't smell slightly dry and recycled.

"June, are you coming?"

Beth hurried past me, brimming with excitement.

With a sigh, I followed her to the passenger lounge. With the exception of the bridge, it was the biggest room on the ship. It was in the very centre of the third floor and most corridors led to it one way or another.

The other women were already in their seats. Beth and I strapped in next to each other. She'd become a friend, despite our different outlooks on what awaited us on Alba. Her enthusiasm had been somewhat infectious. Without her, I may have been firmly in the camp of those who wanted to return home immediately.

I closed my eyes when the ship began to tremble. Eron flashed in my mind, smiling at me. It happened a lot recently. I dreamed of him almost every night. I may have only seen his picture, but in my dreams, I'd heard his voice, seen him move, felt his touch. I tried hard to forget those dreams. They weren't real. In real life, Eron might be completely different. Maybe he was a complete arse. Just because he was drop-dead gorgeous didn't mean his personality matched his looks.

"I hate flying," Beth muttered.

I opened my eyes to look at her. "We've been on a spaceship for a month."

"Yes, but until now, we didn't tumble towards a planet that will kill us if we crash on it."

I reached out and took her hand. "It'll be fine. Captain Ghorr is a good pilot."

"The best," an Albyan male said from behind us. Khar, if I wasn't mistaken. "Just like the Starlight is the best ship in existence. You couldn't be in a safer place, lassies."

I cringed. For some reason, all the guys called us lassies. No matter how often we insisted that they use our names instead, they kept on doing it. If my match - Eron - was going to do the same, I may have to punch him. It was driving me mad.

With one final rumble, the shaking stopped. Bagpipe music blared through the speakers and the males behind us cheered.

"The Albyan planetary anthem," one of them explained.

It was yet another reminder of just how similar our cultures were. I doubted their bagpipes were the same as ours, but they sounded almost the same.

"We have arrived in Priomh, Albya's capital," Captain Ghorr announced. "Welcome to your new home."

The crowd was enormous. At least a thousand red-haired, kilt-wearing men surrounded the spaceship to get a glimpse of us. Fences held them back, thank goodness. Some waved flags, others shouted and flexed their arms as if they wanted to attract us as their mates.

"That's not how it works," Beth snickered.

A human woman came running towards us, followed by a large Albyan with only one slightly crooked antenna. She looked vaguely familiar. That had to be Jenny, the sister of Anna's husband. The Albyans on the Starlight had mentioned her name with awe as if she was some sort of celebrity. Apparently, she'd been the first-ever human mate to an Albyan and the catalyst for the entire operation. Without her, I wouldn't be here. I wasn't sure if I should resent her for it or not.

Instead of coming to a stop in front of us, she continued running and threw her arms around me. "You must be June! Ewan and Anna have told me so much about you!"

"They... have?" I patted her on the back, not quite sure what to do.

"It's so good to see other women again," she said when she stepped back, grinning widely. "Other humans. These guys are all lovely, but I've missed having some girl talks."

I'd had enough girl talk on the Starlight to last me a lifetime. I wasn't a hermit, but I also didn't being surrounded by chatty people all day, every day.

Jenny waved at the other women. "Welcome to Albya. I'm about to have an introductory session with your matches. Two of them were late or we would be done already. My mate suggested it would be fun for you all to watch them, so follow me. Don't jump or run too much, the gravity is slightly different and you might stumble."

In silence, we followed her across the airfield and into a large glass building that reminded me of the armadillo, a big conference centre in Glasgow shaped like the animal. Kind of. Except that it looked more alien. The glass walls of the building turned into screens as we got closer, showing pretty landscapes. Just before we entered through the double doors, the walls turned colourful, forming a green tartan pattern. How very Scottish, I meant, Albyan.

Jenny led us into an airy room. Two males brought refreshments while she fumbled with a device the size of a smartphone.

"Let me," her mate said with a grin and pulled out his own device. He aimed it at the wall and it became a screen, showing a room very similar to this one. Ten Albyan males sat on chairs, their expressions ranging from nervous to excited. That had to be our matches. I searched the room until I found Eron. He was at the very back, the chair next to him empty, as if he tried to put some space between himself and the other men. He was even more stunning in real life. His ginger hair was braided and pulled into a loose ponytail, but some strands had broken loose, framing his angular face. He had both pairs of arms crossed in front of his chest which only highlighted his hard muscles.

His gaze was fixed to the ground, his expression passive. Was he not looking forward to meeting me? My heart sank a little. I understood why some of the males looked anxious, but his expression gave away nothing. Maybe coming here hadn't been his decision. Maybe he'd been tricked into it like I had.

"Alright, I'll head over there and tell them a bit about how to treat human women," Jenny said cheerfully. "I'll try and keep it short. We've got a drinks reception set up in the auditorium and after that, we'll get you to your hotel for the night. Tomorrow, you'll accompany your matches to their homes. If you're comfortable, that is. If you prefer to stay in Priomh for a bit longer, that's fine too. I know these males are strangers to you."

That sounded like a better option to me. I didn't want to be alone with a random guy who may or may not be my soulmate. I still didn't quite believe in that. I was a confident woman and wasn't easily scared, but these males were big and alien. Who knew what their idea of personal space was like. And I certainly didn't want him to jump into my bed.

"Enjoy the show," Jenny grinned and left the room.

6

Eron

I could feel her. My antennae were itching like crazy while also seeming to burn. I kept touching them to make sure they weren't on fire. The other males in the room did the same. It was reassuring that we were all similarly affected by the presence of our females. They had to be close. We'd been herded into this room and hadn't been able to watch their arrival. Jenny was going to give us an introductory talk. Nonsense. Once I'd see my mate, I'd know what to do. Thorrn had spoken of how his antenna - even though he only had one - had led him to his mate when Jenny had been in danger. I was convinced my own appendages would tell me what to do.

I bet my female was aching to be with me. She'd travelled for a long time to come here. That was a sign of how devoted she was to me already. She hadn't expected me to travel to her.

I couldn't wait to embrace her. I'd worry about everything else later. For now, I just wanted her in my arms. My lips on hers. My cock buried deep inside her.

I'd been hard ever since I'd entered this room and felt her presence. It was completely different from how it felt when I touched myself. I'd never fucked a female. The Sleep had happened just when I'd reached maturity and I'd never got the chance. My own hands had been the only way to find relief, but the thought of having her wrapped around my cock was almost too much to bear. How was Thorrn able to leave the house? In his position, I'd spend all day and all night in the bedroom, my female tightly in my arms. I flexed my fingers. Soon, I'd get to hold her.

"Hey guys," Jenny greeted us as she hurried into the room. "Sorry we're starting late. I'll try and keep this fairly short. I know you're all eager to meet your mates."

She spotted me and gave me a little wave. "They're all very excited to meet you. But first, some ground rules. These women have not officially decided to stay on Albya. They signed a contract to come here and stay for a month to meet their matches."

Collective gasps filled the room. There was a chance the females would leave us? My mate would return to her planet?

Hours ago, I'd considered returning home without meeting her. Now, I couldn't imagine not bringing her to my farm and claiming her as my mate. How quickly things had changed.

"I'm sure once they've seen how strapping and lovely you all are, they'll decide to stay," Jenny said with a small laugh. "But you can't put any pressure on them. They're matched to you, but that doesn't mean you can treat them as if they're your permanent mates. Don't expect to get physical right away. Or at all."

Again, some of the males gasped. I had enough self-control to stay silent, even though I wanted to cry out in shock. No physical contact? I didn't think my cock would survive that. Before I'd come to the spaceport, my plan had been to take a look at the female, see if my mating antennae had a reaction, then leave again. Now, I couldn't imagine returning home without her. If she could change my mind and body from a distance, what would it be like once I actually lay eyes on her?

Jenny cleared her throat. "How many of you follow tradition and require a handfasting before you can sleep with your female?"

"With that, she means mating," Thorrn explained drily, his arms crossed in front of his chest. He looked very pleased with himself. "They call it sleeping but trust me, there won't be much sleep for you once you discover the joys of the Peritan female body."

"Shut it," Jenny snapped, but her eyes sparkled with amusement. "Show me your hands.".

Forty hands shot up. I didn't know why we had to do it, but I didn't want to disappoint her. She was the key to meeting my mate.

Jenny laughed out loud. "I need to add that to my list of untranslatable idioms. Put down your hands, that's not what I meant. If you believe in no sex before handfasting, raise *one* hand so I can see."

I wasn't quite sure what to do. My parents hadn't waited for their handfasting, I knew that. But I also didn't want to appear uncivilised. It might give the wrong impression if I admitted that I wanted to fuck my mate right away. Slowly, I raised one arm.

All but one male did the same. He looked around the room, realised what was happening and quickly raised his hand. I chuckled to myself.

"Good," Jenny continued. "All the Elders have agreed to conduct handfasting ceremonies as soon as you and your mates decide you want to take that step. They're willing to travel to wherever you're based. But please don't rush this. Don't pressure your females. It needs to be their decision to commit to a relationship with you, am I clear?"

I nodded. It wasn't going to be easy, but I understood that it was important for my mate to be in control.

Everything was going to be new for her. I was going to be patient and help her adjust to life on Albya. Life with me.

"I've put together a little guide for you to read. It includes everything from what food we humans can eat, what our planet is like, and a bit about our physiology."

"They bleed," Thorrn stage-whispered. "Once every Peritan month. Don't be like me and panic. Don't call a healer. Don't start thinking your mate is dying."

Bleed? That sounded awful. I was glad Jenny and Thorrn had already gone through some of these things. I'd study this guide and learn it by heart this very evening. Bleed. I shuddered.

"It was adorable," Jenny said, shooting her mate an amused look. "I've also been told that the Intergalactic University is working on a guide to humans. As soon as I can get my hands on it, I'll pass it on."

I made a mental note to check out the IGU's latest courses on the quantnet. I'd taken some husbandry modules back when I'd first got into taigeis farming and they had been very helpful. Learning more about my mate and her culture was critical, so I didn't care that the IGU's tuition costs were among the highest in the galaxy. I could afford it.

"Alright, I think we're almost done." Jenny pulled out her commstick and expertly navigated through the complicated menus. I should probably get my mate a commstick too. And a commpad. She would probably want to communicate with her friends or family back on Peritus, so I'd have to find a way for her to do that. Suddenly, there was so much to do and I wished I'd had more time to prepare. I'd been an idiot. Instead of getting ready for my mate, I'd wasted my time debating whether I should come here at all. Sgidding idiot.

"Thorrn and I will be available for advice whenever you need. I know there are some things you'll probably prefer to talk about with another male. Do you have any questions before we let you meet the ladies?"

Yes, I had about a hundred. But I wasn't going to ask them now. I wanted to see my mate.

One young idiot male didn't feel the same way. "I have a question. What if my mate doesn't like me?"

He sounded pitiful. To be fair, I had thought the same thing, but I'd never say it out loud in front of other males.

"My mate's brother says that technically, mates will always have chemistry," Jenny explained. "Depending on what you believe, the two of you are destined to be mates. The stars brought you together, as Thorrn likes to say. Of course, that doesn't mean there won't be difficulties. Our cultures are different. You will have arguments, don't doubt that. It won't be easy. But by now, I believe that if fate and biology say that you have a mate, then you'll be happy together."

Relief flooded me. It was meant to be. The stars hadn't forgotten me. They'd given me a mate.

My antennae tingled painfully. If another male was going to ask a question, I'd strangle him. I needed to see my female before my antennae burned to a crisp.

"Let's get something to drink and meet your mates," Thorrn said impatiently. "As my mate said, you can ask us other questions later."

I was the first male to leave the room. I adjusted my kilt while hurrying after Thorrn, making sure my sporran hung correctly in the centre. It had the stylised emblem of my clan stitched on. I may have become a hermit and didn't see my extended family very often, but I was proud to be part of Clan Monadh. Running a hand through my braided hair, I wondered what my mate would think of me. Would she find me attractive? Had Peritan females the same ideals of beauty as us?

I wasn't pretty - only females were *pretty* - but I had heard that Albyan females had liked strong men with muscular arms. They also preferred cocks with at least four petals. I had six. Not many males had that many. I hoped my mate would appreciate that.

Thorrn led us into the main auditorium, where small hovering trays held drinks. I took a random glass and downed it in one go. I needed the liquid courage.

"Gentlemen, please stand over here with Thorrn!" Jenny shouted. "I'll get the ladies."

"It'll be fine," Thorrn muttered to me when I joined him. "I've seen a picture of your mate. Jenny wouldn't like me saying it, but she's very attractive."

I growled. How had he been able to see my mate and I hadn't?

I wanted to challenge him to a fight - even though I knew I'd lose, after all, he was a professional cage fighter - but that's when Jenny returned to the room, followed by ten females. They were so small. Albyan females were smaller than us males, but the Peritans were quite a bit shorter. It would make carrying her around even easier.

I scanned the group, searching for my mate. My antennae were burning with pain. Hopefully, they'd stop once I got closer to her. I didn't want to be distracted. One female stood out to me right away. She was at the edge of the group as if she didn't quite belong to them. I sympathised. I felt the same way. Her short hair was the same red as mine, maybe a little brighter. She wore an unflattering dress that resembled one of the sacks the taigeis feed was delivered in. It didn't hide her beauty, however. It was a little strange how they all only had two arms. After spending several hours with Thorrn's mate, I should have been used to the sight, but it was still weird. The only Albyans with two arms were amputees. I stared at her chest, relieved to see that she had the correct number of breasts. Having only one wouldn't have been enough for nursing our offspring.

My heart skipped a beat when I realised what I'd just thought. It meant...she was my mate. My antennae tingled with approval. The pain got less in an instant, decreasing to a dumb ache that I could easily ignore.

That was her. My female.

"Laura, you're matched to Khran," Jenny said and a blue-haired female stepped forward. One of the males - one at least ten rotations older than me - ran to her and swept her into his arms. She squealed, not with joy but with alarm.

"Let her go," Jenny commanded sharply. "No touching until the woman initiates it."

Khran gently set her back on her feet and knotted his four hands together in a gesture of apology. Jenny nodded in approval, then looked at her commtab again.

"Beth, you're matched to Obi."

I watched as male after male got to meet their female until only two of us were left.

"Eron, you're matched to June."

Finally. I hurried towards my mate. Her eyes met mine and she stumbled. I moved faster than I ever had before, catching her just before she hit the floor. I pressed her against my chest, breathing in her scent. She smelled like morning dew and nectar. My antennae vibrated, then the pain was gone.

"Mate," I whispered before I kissed her on the mouth.

7

June

I froze when the alien's lips met mine. I should push him away. Jenny had told them that us women had to initiate any physical contact. But he'd also saved me from embarrassing myself. Tripping over my own feet. That was so very me.

He didn't move as if he was waiting for me to either push him away or give into the kiss.

I shouldn't want him. Shouldn't enjoy the way I was pressed against his chest. His four arms were wrapped around me, making me feel strangely safe. Not that I'd felt *unsafe* before, but...

I closed my eyes and opened my lips ever so slightly. That was all he needed. He kissed me as if we were alone in the room. His lips were soft and hard at the same time. His beard brushed against my skin, not as bristly as one of my ex's beards had felt. His tongue nudged my lips open and with a moan, I let him in. This wasn't a first kiss between people who'd only just met each other. I felt like I'd done this before. He seemed familiar, like an old friend who I hadn't seen for many years.

I realised my hands were still held out as if to brace for a fall and I wrapped my arms around his back instead. And then remembered that he was naked from the waist up. Plains of hard muscle waited for me. He worked out for sure.

"That's enough, Eron." Jenny's voice drifted from far away. I ignored her. I didn't want Eron to stop kissing me. I didn't want to leave his embrace. I clung to him and in return, he pulled me even tighter against him. He was hard under the kilt. I could feel him. If we hadn't been surrounded by others, I might have jumped him here and now. I wanted him so much. I'd never desired anyone like this before.

I moaned again, unable to stop myself. His taste filled my mouth, something spicy and exotic. Just like the rest of him. His hands drew circles on my back. I wished I'd worn something more revealing, preferably with an open back so I could feel his hands on my bare skin. Or a shirt that he could slip his hands under. Instead, I'd chosen a shapeless dress. It had been supposed to be a message: I wasn't here for sex. I wasn't going to be a woman about to jump into bed with a stranger.

Yet here I was, jutting my hips against him in a desperate need for release.

Hands landed on my shoulder. Not Eron. We were pulled apart. I opened my eyes, breathing hard. Thorrn had a tight grip on Eron while Jenny was pulling me away from my mate.

"Not the reaction I expected. But I don't want you to do something you'll later regret."

I didn't turn to look at her. My gaze was locked on Eron. An invisible connection held us together, even though our bodies no longer touched.

"I think Cyle would like to know about this," Thorrn said. "None of the others have reacted like this. It might be of some scientific value."

Jenny scoffed. "You sound just like your brother. Let's give them some time alone first. I'm sure June wants to get to know her mate first. They only just met."

It was like a bucket of icy water had been poured over me. My arousal dimmed and I started shaking my head, slowly waking from the dream. Getting to know my mate. Yes. He was a stranger. And I'd kissed him like he was my lover already.

Oh god. I'd behaved like some hussy. I stumbled back, heat flushing my cheeks. I looked to the floor, unwilling to meet anybody's eyes.

"Come with me," Jenny whispered. "Let's get some privacy."

She took my hand and I let her pull me out of the large room and into an empty corridor. I leaned against the wall and pressed my hot cheeks against the cold glass. What I would give for a cold shower just now.

"Are you okay?" Jenny asked. "I know it's all a bit overwhelming."

I didn't want to look at her. I was mortified that she and everyone had seen me behave like that. I'd *moaned*, for goodness sake. That wasn't normal.

She patted my back. "This is new territory for everyone. The Albyans didn't know how they'd react to their human mates and vice versa. What was true for Thorrn and me could be very different for others." She lowered her voice a little. "Did you notice Thorrn only has one antenna? Because of that, we're not the ideal first case of Albyan-human-mating. His instincts may have been different from Albyans who have both antennae. We were all a bit worried how this first meeting between you all would go. Don't worry. We expected much worse."

"Worse?" I croaked.

"I think Thorrn was preparing for orgies," she chuckled. "While I expected general disbelief, women refusing to go with their matches, and then the occasional wild kiss like yours. As I said, it's all new. Did they tell you on the ship what happened to the Albyan females?"

I turned around and nodded. "They fell in some sort of coma a generation ago and haven't woken since."

"Exactly. And many have died. When their mate dies, so do they. This is the first spark of hope Albyans have had since the Sleep began. They were planning for extinction. Now, they have real hope. They'll forgive you anything you do. A little French kiss to greet your mate is an encouraging sign for them, not something to be embarrassed about. If it wasn't for Hot Tatties and me, the males would expect you to do the handfasting ceremony today. They have no doubts whatsoever that you ladies are their mates." She pulled me into a hug. "Don't worry about what happened. It's natural. When I first met Thorrn, I thought I was pregnant because I got so hormonal."

"Really?"

Jenny laughed. "Really. If I'd known about him being an alien, about being his mate, I may have let go of some inhibitions and reacted like you did. Now, shall we return to the others? Or would you prefer to go to your hotel?"

I took a deep breath. "I could do with a drink."

Eron was talking to Thorrn, his back to the door. Instead of going to him, I grabbed a bright green drink from one of the floating trays. They simply hovered in the air as if kept aloft by magic. I supposed I'd have to get used to a lot of new and strange technology here. The style of the building was similar to the interior of the starlight with curved walls and hovering furniture.

I carried my drink to one of the oval benches lining one side of the room. As soon as I sat down, the bench squeezed my arse. I jumped up, staring at the furniture. I was used to chairs that moulded themselves around you from the ship, but this bench had *squeezed* my bum. It had almost felt like hands on my cheeks. No way was I going to sit on it.

Two of the women stood nearby, their males not in sight. They'd been both part of the sceptics, the ones who couldn't wait to get home. It seemed they weren't as attracted to their matches as I'd been. And still was. I risked a quick peek at Eron. He was staring at me from across the room. His top arms were crossed in front of his chest while he held two drinks with the others. He lifted one of the glasses and his lips moved.

I raised my own. "Cheers," I whispered. Instead of going to him, however, I joined the two women.

Sara raised her eyebrows at me. "I thought you'd be in bed with him by now. Or against a wall."

My blush returned in full force.

"Let her be," Lulu admonished her friend. "If my match was as attractive as hers, I may have been tempted to kiss him, too."

Sara gave her a doubtful look but didn't say anything. We drank in silence, but I felt unwanted. On the ship, we'd sometimes talked about our worries and doubts as unwilling alien brides, but it semeed they no longer saw me as one of them. I was now in the camp of those women who were happy to be with their matches. Was I?

I glanced at Eron again. He was still looking at me. Maybe I should have found that creepy, but instead, it just made me all hot and wanting again. Going anywhere near him would've been a bad idea. I'd end up snogging him again in front of every human and alien in the room. No. I'd learned my lesson.

I sought out Jenny. She'd joined her mate who had all four arms wrapped around her. They looked adorable together.

You could have this too, a naughty little voice inside me whispered. And it was right. All I had to do was walk over to Eron and let nature do the rest. He wanted it. I wanted it. Why was I fighting our instincts?

Because it wasn't what I'd signed up to. I didn't like being lied to. It went against my principles and my innate sense of right and wrong. Giving into my desire for Eron would mean the dating agency's shady practises were worthwhile. I didn't want that. They hadn't lied, but they'd omitted a large part of the truth. Because of them, I'd spent a month of my life on a spaceship.

I sighed and signalled Jenny. She kissed her mate on the cheek and danced over to me. "Time to get you to your hotel?" she asked, shooting me a knowing look.

"Aye, I need some alone time."

"No problem." She pulled out her device again and pressed a button. Green holographic lines appeared above it, reminding me of a spiderweb. Jenny moved them around, twisting her fingers as if the hologram was a real object. "I've called one of the volunteers who'll get you to your room," she said after a moment. "We had hundreds of males volunteer to help with organising this first human match visit. He may be a little curious but just tell him no when he asks too many questions. Albyans may be big and slightly scary, but they value a female's wellbeing above everything else."

A young male hurried towards us. He had two golden rings clasped around the bottom of his antennae, with more rings lining his ears and one on his eyebrow. An alien punk. I liked him immediately. Before becoming a boring cog in the world of corporate finance, I'd been a bit of a rebel myself. Not enough to have facial piercings, but I had experimented with dying my hair all the colours of the rainbow.

"How can I help?" the Albyan asked, bowing his head to Jenny and me. "I'm Amsen."

"Could you take June to her room? I've sent you the details already. She wants to retire for the night."

Amsen gave me a curious look. "Of course."

"And make sure she gets some food. I've told the hotel to provide menus in English, but in case they forgot about that, order her a variety platter."

"Aye, Jenny of Clan Lannadh." He looked at her with real reverence. "I will send you a message once I've dropped her off at the hotel."

Amsen gave me a smile and held out all four of his hands. "I believe Peritans like to shake hands as a greeting?"

A roar shattered the conversations around us and a shadow flashed through my field of vision. Amsen was flung back. Before I could see if he was alright, my face was squashed against something hard. And warm. And naked.

Eron.

He wrapped his arms around me as if he wanted to shield me from the world. I felt tiny compared to him.

His grip was so tight that I could barely move my head to look up at him.

"Eron," Jenny chided. "What the fuck?!"

"He wanted to touch her," Eron growled. The words made him tremble and before I realised what I was doing, I was patting his back. He definitely had boundary issues, but in this moment, I didn't care. His touch was what I'd craved. His embrace pushed away all the doubts and worries plaguing my mind. I didn't want him to let me go. I wanted him to keep me in his arms.

It was ridiculous, but I lacked the self-control to push him away.

"Do you want me to get him off you?" Jenny's mate asked, his voice heavy with concern. "I know he'd never hurt you, but if I'd done this to my mate when we first met, she'd have called the enforcers on me. Or kicked me in the balls."

Eron growled again. He was behaving like an animal - and why did I find this utterly sexy? My nipples were hard against his chest. He had to feel them, sense my arousal.

"It's fine," I managed to say.

"You two better get out of here," Jenny said, sounding as if she was trying very hard not to laugh. "Before the other males think they can behave the same way."

"I wish my brother was here to see this," Thorrn muttered. "I hope someone filmed it. I don't know what's keeping him but he'll want to know how you two reacted."

I kind of wanted to correct him, making it very clear that it was Eron who'd reacted like a bear in heat. But then I remembered just how wet I was between my thighs and decided to stay quiet. Wearing a dress had been a bad idea. My panties were soaked and I didn't have a second pair with me. My suitcases were in a hotel and I didn't even know how far it was from here.

"I'm taking her home to Fàsail," Eron stated. "Get her things sent there. I can't stand all the other males."

With that, he lifted me up and ran out of the room, cradling me in his arms as if I was the most precious thing in the universe.

8

Eron

Everyone gave us a wide berth. I suspected Thorrn had warned everyone to stay out of my way and he was right to do so. Every time I'd seen a male getting close to my mate, my antennae had burned with agony. I couldn't stand her being more than an arm's length away from me. Now, she was where she belonged. In my arms, pressed against my chest. My antennae tingled gently, the pain all but gone.

June looked up at me with a strange expression. I should know what she was thinking. She was my mate. But I had no idea how to interpret those slightly widened eyes, the flushed cheeks, the flared nostrils. Her scent muddled my senses. It was the sweetest thing I'd ever smelled and I couldn't get enough of it.

I wondered what she'd taste like. I barely resisted licking her skin. If we'd been alone, I probably would have, but for now, I had to get us to my shuttle. I was glad now that I'd insisted on using my own transport to get to the spaceport and not ride along with Thorrn and his mate. Pit air itaig, why had I parked so far away?

"Where are we going?" June asked when I finally stepped outside the building. "Correction. Where are you going?"

She didn't seem angry, just amused. That was a good sign. She liked being carried in my arms.

I adjusted her slightly so that her hips no longer pressed against my cock. I didn't want to have an accident. My seed would only be spilt inside her, not on my kilt. From now on, my body was hers. I would never touch myself again. She was the only way I'd be able to get rid of this sgidding erection.

"Hello, can you hear me?" She slapped my chest to get my attention.

"Sorry. Uhm. My ship. Home."

My brain wasn't capable of forming longer sentences. She was too distracting. How was I going to look after my taigeis with her around? I'd have to get a sling to tie her to my chest like I'd seen Albyan females do with their offspring before the Sleep. I could carry her around all day, feel her soft skin on mine... It would be torture not to ravish her several times an hour. Oh,

Lady Beyra, why were you testing me? What had I done wrong to be given such temptation?

I stopped in front of a shuttle, realised it wasn't mine, continued on until I finally reached my rusty old transport. I should have cleaned it. Should have repainted the outside. Bought some of the fluffy pillows Thorrn's mate seemed to like.

"Is that yours?" June asked. She tried to turn around to get a better look, but I tightened my grip on her.

"Yes, that's my shuttle. I'm sorry it's nothing like what you're used to. I can get a better one. I'm not as poor as this shuttle makes me look, I promise. I-"

Her hand landed on my mouth.

"I've never seen a shuttle in my life," she said. "So I don't even know what it's supposed to look like. This is more advanced than anything you'd find on Earth. So stop feeling sorry for yourself. It doesn't suit you."

I first stared at her in shock, then threw my head back and laughed. My little mate had spunk. I liked it.

"What about my things?" June asked. "Jenny said they'd be brought to the hotel."

I shrugged. "I'll tell them to deliver your belongings to my farm instead. Do you need anything right away?"

She pursed her lips, then shook her head. "No, I guess I don't. I'd like to change, but it's not important."

For a moment, I considered taking a detour to the hotel, but it would be full of males and I couldn't stand the idea of having anyone near us. The thought itself made me angry. I wanted to punch something to show the world that I would protect my mate, no matter what. She was mine. Forever.

I pressed my hand against the shuttle's side and the door slid open.

"Wow, how did you do that? Is there no key?" June wiggled in my arms. Silly female. As if I'd let her go.

"Palmprint recognition," I explained. "It will only open to my touch."

I climbed up the three steps that had been lowered from the shuttle and climbed into the main cabin. *Stuff* lay all over. Empty food canisters, tools, a broken commstick, even half a bag of taigeis feed. I wanted to put my hands over June's eyes so she wouldn't see the mess. While the cabin would be more comfortable, the cockpit was clean. Ish. It was better than this, anyway.

I carried her into the cockpit, a glass globe that looked a bit like a head attached to the shuttle's ovoid body. I'd long since removed the second chair to make more space for myself and any potential taigeis cub I was hand-rearing. It gave me the perfect excuse to keep her in my lap. I kept my lower arms wrapped around her waist to make it very clear to her that she was to stay in that position. Her arse was pressing onto my cock, but

I'd have to live with that. Better than be parted from her even for a single click.

The door to the cabin slid close as I activated the engines.

"Requesting permission for lift-off," I said while getting the shuttle ready. The air regulator's approval came right away. I could have switched to autopilot, but this was June's first shuttle flight. I wanted her to see what a great pilot I was. I'd earned top marks at the academy and I could have easily got a job in the spaceforce. But then the Sleep had happened and everything changed. Now, the only time I got to fly was when I went to the market or visited my sister. The trip to Priomh was the longest flight I'd done in at least a rotation.

I made the shuttle ascend in a straight line until we reached the lowest allowed altitude. I wanted her to see more of the city now that she wouldn't get a chance to stay the night.

"See that tower over there?" I pointed at the brightly lit building in the shape of a gigantic standing stone. "That's the seat of the Council of Elders. Each Albyan clan has their own government, but when it comes to issues affecting all of Albya, it's the Elders who make the decisions. Every clan has one representative. My father used to represent Clan Monadh until he... anyway."

"It's so tall," June exclaimed. Her eyes were wide with wonder. It made me proud of our capital city and sad that I no longer lived here. "How many people live here?"

"I'm not exactly sure. I think it used to be about a million, but nowadays it depends on whether you count the females or not. The ones who're still alive."

She stilled. "Do you have women in your family who're asleep? Your...mother?"

I looked straight ahead, trying hard to keep my face expressionless. "My mother passed away when my father died. It's something the scientists can't explain. Not that they understand anything about the Sleep. They don't know what caused it, don't have a cure and don't know why females die at the same time as their mates." I took a deep breath to steady myself. It was still hard to remember the moment I'd seen both my parents breathe their very last breath. Their hearts had stopped at exactly the same time. "My sister is still alive. She never found a mate, so for now, she lives."

"I'm so sorry," June whispered. "That must be awful. Does she live with you?"

"No, she's at a facility about twenty clicks from me. I try to visit her at least once a week."

"Twenty clicks, I think that's thirty minutes in our time. They explained it on the Starlight but I keep getting your times mixed up."

"It's about a seventh of the time it'll take us to reach my farm, if that helps." I'd have to read up on Peritan conventions. Hopefully, most of what I needed to know would be in Jenny's guide. If not, I'd contact the Intergalactic University myself.

"Wait, a farm? I thought you ran a business." She didn't sound happy about it.

"I don't know who told you that, but I suppose the farm is my business."

"I can't believe we're going to a farm," she muttered. "Just when I thought things were looking up."

She didn't want to be on a farm. She was disappointed. She'd thought I was something I wasn't. Who the sgidding sgid had given her such wrong information? Although maybe I should be grateful. She sounded like she may not have come with me if she'd known.

"What's the problem?" I asked, fighting hard to keep my voice level. "You don't like farms?"

It took her a moment to answer. "I'm not an animal person. Mostly because I'm allergic to anything furry. And I don't like dirt. Farms are the epitome of dirtiness." June sighed. "But I shouldn't be so judgemental. Alien farms might be different, right?"

"Right," I echoed. "But you don't have to work on the farm. You don't even have to get close to the taigeis. I'll keep them away from you, if that's what you need."

The thought of not being able to share my passion for the taigeis with her hurt, but if that was the price I had to pay, then so be it.

"I'm sorry, I sound like a total bitch. I'm going to try very hard to let go of all my prejudice. I just hope I'm not allergic to your livestock."

"Our medicine is a lot more advanced than yours," I reassured her. "If you do indeed have a reaction to them, we'll find a solution. But I've never met anyone who's allergic to taigeis. To other animals, yes, but those allergies are usually cured in childhood as soon as they're discovered."

"It would be kind of nice to find an animal I'm not allergic to. Besides fish and reptiles. My grandma got me a turtle once, but it was very boring. I wanted to cuddle my pet like other kids did, but of course that didn't work. Maybe that's why I don't like animals much."

She shifted against me and I had to suppress a groan. "You said you used to live here in the capital. Why did you move away?"

I wished I could tell her. One day, I would. I didn't want to have secrets from my mate. But if she knew the truth, she wouldn't sit here, comfortably snuggled against my chest. She'd run. I didn't want her to think me a monster. For now, I'd have to bend the truth.

"I run a taigeis farm and they only thrive in their natural habitat." It wasn't a lie. It just wasn't what she'd asked. "Did they tell you about taigeis on the Starlight?"

"I don't think so. I assume they're some kind of animal?"

"Indeed. For a long time, nobody thought they could be tamed. They're feral and not exactly friendly. Taigeis are small but vicious. Their teeth are sharp enough to rip flesh out of an Albyan's leg. And believe me, I've had plenty of them try."

It wouldn't be long until she saw the scars on my leg. Most of my injuries got healed by the medpod, not leaving a mark no matter how severe, but there had been times when I hadn't got back to the house in time.

"I am the first Albyan to domesticate taigeis," I said proudly. "Currently, my farm houses about two hundred of them."

"I still don't know what exactly they are, but I'm sure that's impressive." June yawned. "Sorry, it's been a long day."

"Then you should sleep." I adjusted the chair, turning it into a recliner. "I'll switch on autopilot so I don't disturb you. I'll wake you when we get there."

"Are you sure?"

I couldn't resist. I stroked her hair, revelling at how soft it was. It was strange how her hair was shorter than mine even though she was a female. I might ask her if she'd let me braid it the Albyan way. It would make it even shorter, but I was sure it would suit her.

"Sleep, my mate," I whispered, pleased when her eyelids fluttered shut. She trusted me enough to sleep in my lap.

I watched as her breathing grew slower. The smallest of smiles curved her lips and I couldn't help but smile myself. Had I ever been happier? I didn't think so.

I closed my eyes and tried to ignore her weight on my cock. This was going to be a long flight.

She'd be the first stranger to stay at my farm. It was dangerous to have her there. My episodes had been increasing recently. It didn't matter if I had one in front of the taigeis. They didn't understand what I mumbled during my seizures. But June would. And as soon as she heard what I'd done, she'd run. I'd be without a mate.

Maybe we should have stayed in Priomh.

9

June

For a moment, I didn't know where I was. I was warm, comfy and surrounded by darkness. The sound of slow, heavy breathing came from my right. Somewhere in the same room but not directly next to me.

I rolled onto my back, examining the memories that slowly flowed through my sleepy mind. The Starlight. Meeting Eron. Sitting on his lap as we travelled to his home. Falling asleep while nestled in his arms. The fact that I was now lying on a bed - or at least something that felt like a soft mattress - meant we'd landed. How did I manage to sleep through that? I never slept this deeply. I must have been tired. Maybe it was the change of atmosphere or gravity. It's not like I'd ever been on a different planet before. Our bodies probably needed lots of energy to adjust to that.

Something moved on the bed, barely making a sound. I sat up straight, instinctively reaching for the light switch above the headboard - except that there was neither a headboard nor a switch. What if it was a snake? Some kind of predator?

"Eron," I whispered.

"Mate?" He responded immediately. Maybe he hadn't been asleep after all. "What's wrong?"

"There's something on the bed."

The lights went on without warning and I squeezed my eyes shut. Way too bright. I blinked only to find a ball of fluff sitting right next to me. It was definitely alive because it was breathing, but what the fuck was it? It looked a bit like a hedgehog that had curled up into a ball, except that it had fur rather than spikes. I didn't feel threatened by it, but what did I know. Maybe it was poisonous.

Eron whistled softly and the fluffball unravelled, revealing a tiny snout below big brown eyes. Those were the kind of eyes that made you all gooey and happy to spoil the animal however much it wanted. Puppies had nothing on this animal. Its snout twitched as it looked around the room.

"Sorry about that," Eron said with a sigh. "I thought I'd closed the door. The cub must have got bored. Do you want me to remove him?"

He got up from a chair. Had he been sleeping on that? I took in my surroundings. I was on a bed, a thin yet warm blanket covering me. I still wore the same dress. The room was circular with several cubby holes built into the stone walls. In some places, the white paint had peeled away, revealing the stone underneath. The place had a rustic feel to it. It was the exact opposite of the futuristic, shiny buildings I'd seen while flying over Priomh.

The little animal squeaked when Eron reached for him and ran onto my lap. He looked up at me, sniffed, then curled up again, hiding his face under all the fur. I'd never seen anything cuter.

"What is it? He?" I asked.

"A taigeis. I told you I had a taigeis farm, right?"

"You did, but I assumed the animals were big, like cows or pigs or something. Not adorable, tiny, cute, fluffy, kissable furballs." I couldn't believe I was talking about an animal like that. I'd never felt so...gooey. And my eyes didn't itch, my throat wasn't closing up and my nose wasn't running. No allergy, unless the symptoms appeared later than they usually did.

Eron laughed. "I have no idea what cows and pigs are, but I know everything there is to know about taigeis. I'll be happy to answer whatever questions you have. But first, are you hungry?"

As soon as he said that, I realised I was starving. When had I last eaten? A light lunch on the Starlight before we'd landed, but I'd been too excited to eat much. There'd been nibbles at the reception, which I'd ignored after that embarrassing incident with Eron. My lips tingled at the memory. I'd never been kissed like that and I couldn't wait to do it again.

"Yes, I could do with some food."

Short hand for 'I'm ravenous and could eat half a cow'.

"How about some taigeis steak? I'm told my steak with caramelised neeps is the best in the entire region."

I stared at him. Was he joking?

"You...eat these?" How could anyone hurt this innocent little fluffball?

"Of course. They're an Albyan delicacy."

"But..." I tentatively stroked the cub's thick fur and it began to purr. Not quite as loud as a cat but just as adorable. No way was I going to eat him.

"Before I set up my farm, taigeis was once of the most expensive dishes. Only few hunters were able to procure wild taigeis and demand for their meat was high. They don't stay as small as this cub is just now. In about a month, he'll start growing his teeth. Adult taigeis have powerful jaws and while they mostly avoid conflict, when they're challenged, they'll bite. Hard."

"I don't care. I won't eat him."

Eron chuckled. He sat on the bed and reached out to pet the cub. Our hands met and a zing of electricity shot through my body, making my hair stand on end. Eron's eyes widened. He must have felt the same thing.

"I want you," he whispered, suddenly very close. "I want to rip that dress off your body. I want to taste you. I want to fuck you. But I'm going to be good and make you food instead." He sighed deeply. "My poor cock will have to stay hard for a little while longer."

I couldn't help it. I laughed.

Eron grinned and took my hand, pressing a kiss to my knuckles. "I'll be back soon."

"But no taigeis," I protested. "Do you have vegetables? Is that a thing?"

"Yes, of course. We have many edible plants on Albya." He sounded adorably proud of that. "I will see what I have in the cooler. If none of what I have is to your liking, we can go to the market tomorrow. Well, today. I think it's past midnight." His smile wavered a little. "Although maybe we shouldn't be in a public place. Even now, with no one nearby, I feel like strangling any male who even thinks about you."

I didn't know what to say to that. He didn't strike me as a violent man, yet I should probably get worried at this point. I was alone with a stranger who'd just admitted that he didn't want me to be around other people. That didn't sound healthy at all.

"I think it gets better after the handfasting," Eron muttered. "But I should ask Thorrn. And his brother Cyle will want to speak to us. I got a message from him during the flight. He's a scientist and wants to know why we...reacted as we did."

"I've heard of him. He's the one who discovered that Albyans and humans are compatible, right?"

Eron nodded. "He's a friend. I grew up with him and Thorrn. I might be able to stand being in the same room with those two. Maybe." He rubbed his antennae, looking very uncomfortable. "I'm usually in control. I don't like feeling like this. Like I'm an explosion waiting to happen."

He sighed and straightened to his full height, towering above me. He was still wearing his kilt. It magically drew my gaze. I wondered what he was hiding under there. And would I be brave - or stupid - enough to find out?

While he was gone, I stroked the little taigeis between what I thought was its ears. There were tiny nubs above his eyes that could either turn into horns, antennae or ears. Or something else entirely. I'd got to see some of the planets' animals in the films they'd shown us on the Starlight. Many of them had the same antennae as Albyans, so maybe the taigeis would have grow those, too.

"I'm not going to eat you," I promised the cub. "And I'm not going to eat one of your relatives either. You're safe. And if that evil male tries to hurt you, he'll have to go through me."

The little animal looked up at me and yawned, exposing a surprisingly big mouth. Its gums were toothless, but I was beginning to understand what Eron had said about them biting. I couldn't wait to see what an adult taigeis looked like. If the cub hadn't been nestled on my nap, I'd have got up to explore Eron's house and farm, but he was too cute to disturb. It would have to wait until later. Eron had said it was after midnight, so not the best time to explore anyway. I'd stopped wearing my watch on the Starlight because the Albyan day was just over twenty-six hours. The room was windowless, so that didn't help with telling the time either.

I looked up. Now that the light was on, I realised that the ceiling wasn't stone like I'd assumed. It was made of the same glass Albyans used everywhere, with external shutters hiding the sky.

"Do you want to eat in bed or come into the lounge?" Eron called.

Curiosity won over the taigeis cub's cuteness.

"Sorry," I muttered and gently lifted him off my lap. "You can sleep on the bed while I'm gone. You'll get more cuddles later."

He gave me a sad look that almost made me reconsider. I turned around and hurried out of the bedroom before those big needy eyes could change my mind. Another circular room awaited me, this one a little less rustic than the bedroom. Two sofas hovered above the ground, adding something futuristic to the traditional stone walls. The floor was covered in carpets showing a range of Celtic-looking designs. Lots of knots and mythical animals. Not very practical, but pretty. Eron entered from the opposite side, carrying two large trays. Having four hands really came in handy. Yes, that pun was totally intended and almost made me laugh out loud.

"Press your hand against the wall over there," he instructed. "I should have done this before getting the food."

The wall he'd nodded at was made from metal rather than stone. A large screen took up half of it, showing a gorgeous landscape that reminded me of the Scottish Highlands except that the colours weren't quite right. I held my hand against the wall without a clue what I was supposed to be doing.

The metal vibrated, then a part of it split off and slowly lowered itself until it formed a table. It hovered slightly, as if it was deciding where to float, then stilled. The wall where it had come from looked just like it had before. As if nothing had happened. This was technology I couldn't even begin to understand.

"Nice," Eron said while placing the trays on the table. "I programmed the house to accept your palm print. I don't have as much tech as other people, but the few gadgets I do have are quite nifty."

"What else is there?" I asked.

"Let me think... I don't use most of it. All the nanomet walls have inbuilt screens. Some of them aren't usually activated, but if you want to watch something when they're turned off, just press your palm against them. I've also got the latest cleaning tech in my relief room. I'd never get all the dirt off me otherwise." He grinned. "Taigeis aren't the cleanest of animals. They produce a lot of...dirt."

"The relief room is the bathroom, I assume?"

"Yes, I have a bath. Do you like taking baths? The tub is big enough for both of us."

My cheeks flushed. He'd brought the conversation into very dangerous territory. The thought of being in a bathtub with him, naked, made me squeeze my thighs together. How did he manage to make me aroused with just a few words? It wasn't fair.

"Let's eat," I said.

He smirked, knowing very well why I'd changed the topic.

I looked around for chairs. The sofas were a little too far from the table. "Do we eat standing?"

Eron frowned. "Is that what Peritans do?"

"No, I just asked because there aren't chairs."

"Ah. Sit on the floor and you'll see."

I gave him a curious look, then shrugged and sat down on the rug. As soon as my bum hit the fabric, it pushed against me, raising me up until it felt like I was sitting on a thick pillow.

As soon as Eron sat opposite me, the table lowered itself until it hovered only a foot above the floor.

"It saves space," Eron explained. "The house was a lot smaller when I first moved here. Just the bedroom, the lounge and a tiny relief room. I've added more to it since, but I've kept the intelligent carpets."

"Intelligent carpets," I muttered. What a strange world I'd been transported to.

I ran my hand over the rug next to me. It didn't move, behaving just like a carpet should.

"If I lie down, will it turn into a bed?" I asked.

"Yes. And if you spread your arms and legs, it'll turn into a cross shape." His eyes bored into mine. "I would very much like to see you with your legs spread."

My core throbbed in response to his words. "Do you always think about sex?"

Eron laughed. "Very rarely, actually. Only since I met you. Now I can't think of anything else. But you need to eat or you won't have any strength for when we mate."

When. Not if. He had no doubts that we'd end up in bed. To be fair, neither had I. And I was okay with that. I might think differently in the morning, but tonight, I was prepared to give in to my urges.

Eron pointed at one of the bowls containing small green balls reminding me of oversized peas or maybe olives. "Try these. They're the seeds of a plant found only in this region. They make a great snack when dried, but they're even better cooked."

Since he'd not given me any cutlery or even a plate, I took one of the balls straight from the bowl. I gave it a sniff. Not much of a smell, maybe a faint note of paprika.

"It's safe, I promise you." Eron was watching me with a wry grin. "There are only a few things on Albya that might not agree with your Peritan digestion. All of the dishes on this table are perfectly edible."

I nibbled on the ball. At first, all I tasted was salt, then something else took over. Goat's cheese. Very mature goat's cheese. It was kind of tasty but too intense to eat more than one or two of.

"You don't like it," Eron said, sounding sad.

"No, it's alright. But I don't think it'll be my favourite."

He picked up a triangular fruit - at least I thought it was a fruit - and held it out to me. I reached for it, but he shook his head, grasped my hand and pulled me halfway over the table.

He held the fruit to my lips. It was warm, not cold as I'd expected.

"What-" The instant I opened my mouth to speak, he pushed in the fruit, feeding me. I took a bit and sweetness exploded within my mouth. Caramel, maple syrup, treacle, fudge, all mixed together. This was a dentist's nightmare. It melted when I tried to chew it, turning into a thick liquid.

"Mmmhm, this is-" He made me take another bite. And another, until his sticky fingers were all that remained, still touching my lips as if waiting. I met his gaze and stuck out my tongue, licking his fingers clean. Eron groaned and pushed past my lips until I was sucking on his fingers. I closed my eyes, imagining that this was something else. My nipples hardened, pushing against my bra.

"What are you doing to me?" Eron whispered huskily. "How do you have such power over me?"

I could have asked him the same. He pulled out his fingers, then rammed them into my mouth again as if he was fucking me for real. Heat bloomed in my core. The emptiness returned, a desperate need to be filled. By him. I needed him.

"Sgid it," he groaned and pulled away his hand. Before I could complain, he was on top of me. I blinked open my eyes just in time to see the table float away, giving us space. His lips found mine and I closed my eyes again, giving myself to the sensations assaulting my senses. He wrapped two of his arms around me, holding me in place, while he used the other pair to keep us halfway upright. He kissed me like he was starving. His beard brushed against my skin like a gentle caress. But Eron's kiss wasn't gentle in the slightest. He was claiming me.

And I was loving it. I hugged him, clinging to him to make sure he didn't go anywhere. I needed him to continue this kiss. Needed to feel his lips, his tongue. Needed to breathe in his scent.

My nails scratched along his back, but he didn't complain. In fact, he growled and nipped my bottom lip. Pain mixed with pleasure. I was floating, clinging to my raft. He was everything.

Until he broke the kiss and said, "I can't."

10

Eron

It was the hardest thing I'd ever done in my life. Pulling back from her physically hurt. But I knew that if I went any further, I'd end up embedded deep inside her. I wouldn't be able to stop. And when I climaxed...

She'd find out everything. I had a seizure almost every time I came. I didn't care when I was on my own, when I stroked myself, imagining it was a female's hands around my cock. But now, June was here. I couldn't let it happen.

But wait, I had an excuse. I'd raised my hand when Jenny had asked who still believed in the tradition of handfasting. That meant I was bound to my actions. I couldn't mate with June until we were officially recognised as mates. I may have broken that rule in other circumstances, but it gave me a good enough reason until I figured out what to do.

"Why?" June whispered. "What's wrong?"

I was glad she'd not asked if she'd done something wrong. She was confident in herself. I loved that.

"There's an old Albyan tradition," I began, but she interrupted me.

"Handfasting. Yes, they explained it to us. Why is it so important? Why can't we sleep together like the adults we are? I consent, you consent, that's it."

I balled all four hands into fists. "I wish I hadn't raised my hand. It was a mistake. I'm sorry."

She sighed and straightened her dress. "I suppose I should be impressed by your self-control. I wouldn't have been able to stop." Her cheeks were flushed, the red almost drowning out her freckles. Her lips were swollen and that sight made me want to kiss her once again. There was no rule against kissing before handfasting. The tradition said no mating...

I grinned. There were many other things we could do that didn't involve burying myself inside her. I could please her in other ways. I'd make her forget all about mating. And I'd get rid of my painful erection once she was asleep, locked in the relief room so she couldn't hear what I muttered during the likely seizure.

"Lie on your back," I whispered.

She cocked her head to the side. "Why?"

"Because I realised that I can worship you in other ways."

Her eyes widened before she smiled. Her tongue flicked across her lips. I would kiss her again soon, but first, I needed to see more of her. The dress hid way too much of her body.

She lay back and the carpet immediately adjusted itself to support her. I was tempted to rip her dress to pieces, revealing her that way, but I was trying to be civilised. Forcing myself to be slow, I gently pushed up her dress, exposing her upper thighs. Holding the dress with my upper hands, I caressed her legs with my lower ones, amazed at how soft her skin was. I couldn't resist licking it. It tasted just as sweet as her scent. Morning dew. The smell of a field of fraoch after rain when the flowers opened their petals and released their fragrance into the humid air.

I kissed and licked my way up her legs, rewarded with small moans that made my cock jerk against my kilt.

"Stop teasing," June moaned.

She tried to reach for me, but I evaded her grasping hands. It wasn't time yet for her to be in control. This was all about me making her feel good.

I lifted the dress a little higher until I got to a flimsy undergarment. I ripped it apart, ignoring June's protest, and finally exposed what I'd been dreaming of during our flight. Her pussy was glistening with arousal, ready to be worshipped. She looked a little different from what they'd taught us in anatomy lessons at the academy: A deep valley was hidden between two mounds, curls of soft hair framing them. So beautiful. I pushed her legs apart a little further, giving me an even better view. Her clit was swollen, peeking out from the valley.

"Touch me already!" June panted and pushed her pelvis up, a clear invitation. How I wished I could mate with her. Plunge into her depths. Make her mine.

But this wasn't the time. I had to be patient.

I lay on my belly, my face above her pussy. Her scent was intoxicating. I couldn't hold back any longer. I licked all along her pussy, lapping up her wetness. Her taste filled my mouth, a drug I was about to get addicted to. I licked her again, delighted when she moaned, before experimenting further with what I could do to her. Whenever I hit a particularly sensitive spot, she would writhe under my touch. I had a tight grip on her thighs, holding her in place, but I enjoyed her struggling. When I sucked on her swollen clit, she screamed. Knowing I could give her such pleasure made me feel powerful. I was going to show her that I was the right male for her. I'd make her forget about everything and everyone. All she'd be able to think of was me, my touch, my tongue in her most sacred place.

"Don't stop!" she screamed. "I'm so close!"

But I didn't want her to come yet. I still had so much more to explore. I pulled back, smiling at her frustrated groans. She was even wetter now. Her sweet nectar was running down her thighs and onto the carpet. It was a waste, but as much as I loved her pussy, I needed to see the rest of her.

"Let's get rid of this dress," I muttered hoarsely.

"Don't rip it," she warned me and pulled it up her body before I could do it for her. The fabric pooled around her neck, her beautiful breasts beneath it now on full display. Her nipples were as erect as my cock. Would she like me touching them? Only one way to find out.

I swirled my fingers around the base of her breasts, taking my time, slowly working my way upwards. When I reached her nipples, I gently squeezed them between two fingers, amazed at how hard they were. I pulled on them ever so slightly. June's moans and whispered curses were my reward. Teasing her was becoming my new hobby. But I needed to taste her again. I took one of her nipples into my mouth. I didn't know why it felt so amazing. I sucked on it, pulling up her breast. How she groaned with pleasure. I closed my eyes and simply focused on the sensation of playing with her body. I ran my hands over her skin, dipped my fingers between her thighs to get another taste of her nectar, before kissing her hard. She was putty beneath my hands, reacting to my every touch. I'd never played a musical instrument, but I imagined this was what it was like. Knowing exactly which spot created what sound. Recognising her by touch alone.

"If you don't let me come, I'm going to murder you," June gasped.

I chuckled. "Say please."

She didn't hesitate. "Please."

I positioned myself between her thighs once more. My cock strained against my kilt and it took every bit of self-control to keep it there.

June looked at me with flushed cheeks and pure need in her eyes. I could have simply sat here and enjoyed the view for days. But she deserved to get the climax she was so desperate for.

Ever so slowly, I pushed a finger into her swollen pussy. It slid in easy, helped by all the wetness, and I slipped in a second. She was so tight.

"Next time, it will be my cock," I promised before I started fucking her with my fingers. She writhed on the floor and only my strong hold on her kept her from escaping. Her sounds became more and more animalistic. When my thumb touched her clit, she screamed.

She was ready for me, but I decided that I didn't want it like that. I needed to be closer. I stopped rubbing her clit and instead went down on my stomach again so I could reach her more easily. Her scent was killing me. I took a deep breath before burying my face between her legs. I sucked, licked, swirled my tongue around her clit. And then she came, her juices shooting into my mouth, her inner muscles taking hold of my fingers, constricting around them. I almost came myself at the thought of her milking my cock like that. I kept suckling her clit until June finally stopped shaking.

She had her eyes closed, her expression serene. I licked my fingers before getting a wet cloth to clean her. She mumbled something, only half-awake. I carried her to the bedroom so she could rest while I went to the relief room to take care of my aching cock. I woke on the floor, my body hurting all over from the seizure I'd had. I was glad I'd decided not to mate with June today. If I'd had the fit while fucking her, she might have discovered my secret. Instead of waiting for me in our bed, she'd be on the next shuttle back to Priomh.

I sighed and returned to the bedroom. June was sleepy but awake. I spooned her from behind, holding her tight. I never wanted to let go of her again.

We didn't sleep right away. We talked in hushed voices, her telling him about my life on Earth, me asking questions. When she got too tired, I put a finger on her lips, silencing her. I felt her smile before she relaxed in my arms, drifting off to sleep.

11

June

I was so very tempted to stay in bed. Eron was spooning me from behind, one of his hands on my stomach, another on my hip. He'd taken off his kilt at some point. I wanted to turn around and continue where we'd started off last night, but I didn't want to tempt Eron into breaking the tradition he'd vowed to uphold. It was kind of adorable how he felt he had to do the honourable thing. I would have preferred him to be a rebel.

Something hopped onto my leg and I wasn't surprised in the slightest to see the taigeis cub making his way to me. It had tiny claws hidden beneath all the fluff and I was glad a thin blanket was between them and my bare skin. I'd never asked Eron if the cub had a name. If he was meant to be eaten, he likely didn't have one. I shuddered.

"Nobody is going to eat you," I reassured him as he snuggled against my cheek. He smelled of heather, that strangely coconut-like scent that I associated with family holidays in the Highlands. I'd never quite decided whether heather smelled of coconut, vanilla or a mix of both. It was most fragrant in the sun and walking along a heather-lined path on a sunny day was a feast for all senses.

"He's not for eating," Eron yawned from behind me. He kissed the back of my neck. "He'll be sold as a pet or become part of the breeding programme if he turns out to be a particularly strong male."

I grinned. "Only strong males get to breed?"

Eron slid his hand up my belly and cupped my breast. "On this farm, yes," he whispered. A pleasant shiver ran down my back. Oh, how I wanted him. But I had to be strong and resist the temptation.

"Want to show me the farm?" I asked and sat up before he could tease me even more.

He sighed. "I want to show you so many other things. But yes. Let's take a tour of your new home. Are you hungry?"

"Starving. It's not like we did much eating last night before...you know."

Eron jumped out of bed, looking guilty. "I'm sorry. I'm a bad mate. I'll prepare you a morning meal while you get dressed."

"Wait," I called when he hurried out of the room. "Do you have any clothes I can borrow? I don't have my baggage and I don't really want to wear yesterday's dress."

He returned and opened one of the cubby holes built into the stone walls to reveal a screen. "This is the fabricator's terminal. Just enter whatever you want and it'll create it within a few clicks. The fabricator's production module is in the storeroom, though, so you may have to walk there naked." He winked at me. "Maybe I shouldn't have shown you the terminal. Maybe I should make you walk around naked all day. I'd like that."

"Are you sure you could resist breaking your no-sex-before-handfasting rule if I was nude the entire time?"

He sighed. "Aye, you're right. I better put on a kilt then. I don't want to tempt you because I know you'll tempt me back." He growled in frustration. "Pit air itaig, why am I such an idiot? I made this so hard for both of us."

I got up and hugged him. Our naked bodies fit together perfectly. I breathed in his scent. It made me feel like I was home. I was safe with him.

His cock hardened against me. Eron gently pushed me back, regret painted across his face. "I think it's better if

I put on my kilt and you create some clothes for yourself. And then we'll have the morning meal before I'll show you around the farm."

The taigeis cub squeaked, reminding us of his presence. Eron grinned. "Yes, you'll get your morning meal, too."

The fabricator terminal was pretty intuitive to operate and a few minutes later, I'd settled on a design. Loose, practical clothes that were appropriate for being on a farm. As much as I wanted to look sexy for Eron, the tiny speck of logic still remaining in my hormone-addled brain insisted on trousers and a shirt instead of the short dress I'd seen in the catalogue. I had to guess when it came to sizes. Of course, the sizing I was used to didn't exist here. They had neither feet, inches, metres or centimetres. I found an option called 'small', which was probably the one to choose. Compared to Albyans, I was tiny. I didn't know how tall Albyan females were, but I assumed they'd be bigger than human women.

The relief room was the next challenge. I'd used the toilet last night which was simple enough, but I couldn't get the shower to work. If it even was a shower. I'd have to ask Eron later, but I was too hungry to experiment with it much further. Instead, I used the large washing basin for a quick sponge bath - minus the sponge. There were no towels. I was probably missing some amazing high-tech way of drying my skin, but again, I couldn't be bothered. I'd just have to wait until I was dry.

Eron was in the lounge, the hover table laden with food. His eyes widened when I stepped into the room.

"Sgid, you're so beautiful," he muttered. "Lady Beyra has blessed me."

I was curious about that Beyra woman he'd mentioned several times already. A deity, I assumed. But I was naked and there was a slight draught in the room, making my gooseflesh rise. This wasn't the time for questions about Albyan belief systems.

"Where's that storeroom?" I asked.

"Over there, but I already collected your clothes from the fabricator." He pointed at a pile on one of the floating sofas. "They're very bland."

Well, that was one way of telling me he didn't like my choice. How rude. "I thought it would be best to get something dark so dirt won't show on it."

"You're expecting to get dirty?"

"You live on a farm," I countered. "You mentioned taigeis shit. I don't expect to stay inside and twiddle my thumbs. I want to see what your life is like."

He rubbed his antennae, looking taken aback. "You actually want to work on the farm? I didn't think any female would want such a life. I used to live in the city with all the conveniences. It was hard to adjust to life here. I assumed you'd find it similarly difficult."

"Yes, I'm a city girl," I said while putting on my clothes. "And I should warn you, the last time I was on a farm was on a primary school trip. I had to go home early because my allergies were playing up. I kind of liked seeing the animals, but not the mud or the smell. But I'm a grown woman now. I can jump over my shadow. Especially for..."

My mate, I wanted to say. But something stopped me from uttering the words. I sighed. "Anyway, we were told to stay with our matches to experience their lives first-hand. If I want to make an informed decision, I need to know what you do all day."

"Informed decision," he repeated, his smile disappearing. He turned around, hiding his face. I knew I'd made a mistake. But it was the truth. As much as my body craved Eron, I couldn't just pretend that I was ready to live on an alien planet for the rest of my life. Couldn't he see that? I'd met him yesterday. We were strangers.

And I wanted him so much.

I cursed my traitorous body. I couldn't think while I was staring at his broad back, his muscled thighs, his kilt - especially now that I knew what he had underneath it.

Urgh. Why was life so hard? For a moment, I wished I'd never signed up to Hot Tatties. But then I wouldn't have met him. My match. I would have stayed ignorant. Never meeting my soul mate, if Pam was to be believed. If I'd been a comic character, my head would have started smoking. My thoughts were all over the place.

"Jenny," I muttered. "Can I talk to Jenny?"

Eron turned back to me, his expression unreadable. "Of course. I'll send her a message. But first, you need to eat."

We ate in silence. I didn't ask what any of the dishes were. Some tasted good, others horrendous. After trying most of them, I settled on a bowl of purple porridge. At least that's what I called it. For all I knew, it could have been squashed taigeis brains. Hopefully not.

As soon as he was done, Eron pulled out his commstick. He still hadn't said a single word. The silence was thickening around me, making me uncomfortable. But I'd not done anything wrong. And I shouldn't have to explain myself to Eron. He'd said that he'd only found out about me a few days before I'd arrived. It was all new to him, too. He couldn't expect me to simply accept that I was his mate and give up the life I'd had on Earth. I'd been fired, yes, but I could have got a new job. I had friends there.

That reminded me, I should ask him if I could somehow speak to Anna. She always had the best advice. And I assumed that she knew about Albyans. Her sister-in-law was with one, after all. During our time on the Starlight, I'd been furious at her for not telling me. By now, I'd concluded that she'd not been allowed to. And that she'd had my best interests at heart. She'd found her own soul mate in Ewan, Jenny's brother. If I'd had a husband like him, I'd want my friends to have an amazing relationship like that, too.

"Cyle will come here later today," Eron announced without looking at me. "He wants to run some tests. He'll bring Jenny along unless you want to talk to her on the quantnet now?"

"No, later is fine. Thank you."

"Then I shall clean the stables and give you some time to make an *informed decision.*"

He sounded so hurt that I wanted to reach out, cuddle him, tell him that I wanted to stay - but I couldn't. Instead, I nodded and averted my gaze.

Eron touched the table and it floated upwards before slowly drifting out of the room, probably to the kitchen. Did the dishes do themselves? Now that was something I could get behind on. A squeak from the direction of the bedroom reminded me of the taigeis cub. He still hadn't been fed.

"Can I feed him?" I asked, surprising myself.

"There's a bottle in the cooler. But be careful, he's greedy and you don't want to get bitten. Maybe I should do it."

"No," I snapped. I didn't know why he made me so angry. "I'll do it."

"Suit yourself." He stormed out of the room. If the door hadn't been a sliding one, I bet he would have slammed it shut.

I picked up the cub from the bedroom, cradled him in my arms and wished he could tell me what to do.

12

Eron

Shovelling shit was exactly what I needed. My muscles strained, distracting me from my anger and fear. It was hard to admit it to myself, but it was mostly fear. I was afraid that June would leave me. That I'd be alone forever. Until I'd met her, I'd been fine with that idea. Now, I'd tasted the possibility of a happy future. Losing her would break me.

Clearly, she didn't feel the same. She had doubts. I'd thought she wanted me as much as I desired her. But no, she wanted to *consider her options*. She hadn't decided that she was going to stay. She might leave me.

I spat on the dirty stable floor, but the foul taste remained. A taigeis came running, probably about to beg for food.

"Go away!" I roared. The taigeis jumped in fear before shooting off around a corner. I instantly felt bad about scaring the animal. I'd spent years getting them to trust me. Some days, it had seemed impossible. I'd spent many nights in the stables, sleeping close to them, proving that I trusted them not to hurt me. Trust went both ways.

I froze. *Trust went both ways.* Maybe that was the answer. I dropped the shovel and hurried to the faucet to wash my hands. I should have gone to the relief room to properly clean myself, but I knew that I might change my mind if I delayed.

I rushed into the house. "June?"

"I'm here," she said quietly and got up from the floor where she'd been sitting with the taigeis. "What's wrong?"

"I need to tell you something. And I need to do it now. I know it's hard, but I want you to promise me that you'll hear me out. Listen to the whole story. And if you want me to call you a shuttle when I'm done, then so be it."

My heart ached at the very thought, but I wouldn't blame her if she wanted to leave. I wouldn't even blame her if she called the authorities. Perhaps it was time to face responsibility for what I'd done.

"You're scaring me a little," June whispered. "But I promise that I will listen."

She sank back to the floor and the rug rose up to meet her, shaping into a seat.

"Sit down," she said. "I'm all ears."

This was my last chance to back out. I clenched my fists. Very instinct was telling me to run.

"Hey, big guy," June suddenly said. Her gentle voice wrapped around me like a soothing blanket. "You can do it."

There was no doubt in her eyes as she looked up at me.

I took a deep breath and knelt in front of her. I stared at the rug while trying to figure out how to start. She waited patiently until I cleared my throat.

"There's a reason why I live here," I began. "I tell people that I always wanted to be a farmer, that moving to the farm was fulfilling a dream, but that's a lie. I didn't move here because I wanted to. I fled. I hid. I pushed everyone away."

I was going in the wrong direction. She didn't need to know how I'd turned the farm into a prison of my own making.

"I have a medical condition. I get seizures. And they make me say things. Blurt out what I'd never tell anyone. And I don't want you to find out that way. I need you to hear it from me while I'm of sound mind."

June looked like she was about to say something, but I shook my head. "No, that's not what's important. I don't care about being ill. Well, it's sgidding inconvenient, but...aaargh." I was so close to getting up and running. I couldn't do it. I just couldn't.

"Would it help if you wrote it down?" she asked gently.

"No. I need to say it. I..." I clenched my hands around my antennae, the pain clearing my mind long enough for me to grind out the all-important words. "I killed someone."

I refused to look at her. I didn't want to see her reaction. I couldn't bear to see the fear in her eyes as she stared at me like the monster I was.

"Tell me. I feel like there's more to the story." Her voice was calm. It gave me the strength to continue.

"I killed a male. Murdered him. And I don't even regret it. I feel no guilt for taking his life. There it is. The truth. I've never told anyone. And I'll never say those words again."

A warm hand clasped mine. I looked at her in surprise. She'd not run. She was still here. And she was holding my hand.

"Why?" she asked simply.

"Does it matter? Isn't the result the same? A dead body, hidden away, never found. It doesn't matter why."

"It matters to me."

I felt like I was falling apart. Breaking into pieces right in front of her. It hurt, it hurt so sgidding much.

"He worked at the facility where my sister is cared for. I found him trying to...I didn't think. I grabbed him, pulled him off her bed, strangled him. And when he was dead, I beat his body. I kicked him, crushed his ribs, wishing I could kill him all over again." I looked her straight in the eyes. "That's the kind of male I am. A murderer."

She didn't speak for what felt like an eternity. But she never let go of my hand. Her warmth seeped through my skin and right into my heart. Having said those words, spoken them out loud, had ripped open an old wound that had never healed. It had been seeping poison into my soul for rotations.

"You defended your sister." June's voice was slightly shaky. "He was trying to hurt her. You protected her from harm."

I couldn't reply. The memory flashed in front of my eyes. I could remember every detail, from the song playing in the background to the tea stain on her bedside table. She'd looked just as serene as always. Dòiche always seemed as if she was half-smiling in her sleep. I prayed that she wouldn't remember what had happened once she woke up. I wouldn't want her to carry that burden.

"What would have happened to him if you'd handed him over to the police?"

"There would have been a trial. That was about a rotation before they changed the law. When I killed him, it was still the old laws. He'd have spent time in a correction facility. Not long because he hadn't succeeded in hurting her. I'd stopped him just in time."

"And what would the new law have said?"

I shook my head. "It doesn't matter. I killed him. It's the worst crime and I'm guilty."

"We were taught your laws on the Starlight," June said, almost a whisper. "I know that if a male hurts a female, his life is forfeit. Anyone who witnesses it can execute the sentence. I thought it was a cruel law, but after hearing your story, I think I've changed my mind. Your sister was defenceless. All your females are while they're trapped in the Sleep. If this had happened a year later, you wouldn't have committed a crime."

"But I did," I insisted. "And I have to pay for it."

"By forcing yourself to be alone? No, if you really wanted to make up for it, you'd hand yourself in to the police and go to prison. That would be justice. What *you* want is to suffer. That's different. The only person who can absolve you is yourself. I can't do that."

I gently removed her hands from mine and got to my feet. "I know. And I'm sorry. I'll call you a shuttle."

She grabbed my ankle before I could move away. "Don't you dare!" She jumped up and faced me, her arms on her hips. She was so much smaller, yet she was burning with emotion that rivalled my own.

"You don't tell me when to leave and when to stay. It's my decision. I'm sick and tired of people making decisions for me." She huffed. "I'm going to stay. You're my mate. And I don't care what you did. You've paid for it by forcing yourself to suffer for years. In my book, that's worse than whatever you would have been sentenced to. Now it's time to let go of the past and start anew."

"You..." My voice broke and I had to clear my throat. "You want to stay? With me? After all that I just told you?"

"You're my mate. I thought I could ignore that, but I can't." She laughed, but it wasn't a happy sound. "I hate that it took you showing me your pain to make me realise that. I wish you didn't have to go through all that. I wish that vile man had never tried to hurt your sister. But it's the past. I want to be your future." Her shoulders dropped. "If you want me, that is."

"Want you?" I repeated dubiously. "*Want* you?" I picked her up and hugged her to my chest. "I don't just *want* you. I *need* you. I desire you like nothing else. I can't imagine being without you. And I want to make you my mate right here, right now."

"No handfasting?" A smile curved her lips as she looked up at me. "Are you sure?"

"I've never been more certain in my life. Unless you want to do the ceremony? I can wait. I understand if you want to make it official."

June laughed. "Nobody is saying that we can't do the ceremony *after* we've mated, as you call it."

"What do you call it?"

"Sex. Fucking. Making love."

"Making love," I repeated. "I like the sound of that."

13

June

He carried me into the bedroom. This was becoming a theme. Would I ever get to use my own legs again? I chuckled.

"What's so funny?" he asked.

"You keep carrying me. Is that an Albyan thing or an Eron thing?"

"It's a me thing. Although Thorrn mentioned that he does the same. I can't help it. I see you and I need to have you in my arms. It's where you belong."

It was strangely romantic. Back home, I would have never let a man carry me. I would have kneed him in the balls if he'd tried. But with Eron, it was different. His four arms were perfect for cradling me against his body and he was strong enough to carry me without breaking a sweat. I was still planning to protest from time to time, but I was starting to enjoy it. The fact that his broad chest was naked only added to the experience.

He gently sat me onto the bed. "I'm so glad that you now have to take off those hideous clothes," he said with a wide grin. "I told you, you should walk around naked. It saves me from having to undress you."

"They're practical," I muttered, but I secretly agreed with him. "Does that mean you'll take off my clothes for me?"

He shot me a predatory look. "No. I'm going to rip them off your body."

And he did. I hadn't thought it possible, but when he grabbed the fabric of my shirt with all four hands, he managed to tear it apart. I gasped when cool air hit my skin. My nipples grew hard and my breasts ached with need.

Eron pushed the remains of the shirt down my arms and flung them across the room. "Next time, I'll use the fabricator for you," he said with a satisfied smile.

"You're going to tell me what to wear?" I spluttered. "No way."

"I'm going to strongly suggest what you wear by destroying any other clothes you may have."

"That's not how things are done," I protested, but he put a finger to my lips, silencing me.

"Let me have my fun, leannan. I promise I will behave once we've finally mated. Until then, I can't control myself. My antennae are burning. My cock is so hard it hurts. And there you are, teasing me with your beautiful body. I need you, June. I need you now."

I looked him straight in the eyes. "Then take me. Don't hold back. Don't you dare hold back."

That was all he needed. In a flash, he'd torn off my pants. I wasn't wearing anything underneath. Mostly because I hadn't found patterns for underwear in the fabricator terminal, but also because I'd hoped for this to happen. Last night had given me a tiny taste of what Eron could do. Now, I'd get to take all of him.

He knelt at the edge of the bed and pushed my legs apart. As soon as his lips touched me between my thighs, I moaned, threw my head back and clung to the sheets. I thought it had been amazing before. No. There was no comparison. It was as if he'd used last night as a lesson to learn precisely what motion elicited the strongest response. He licked my clit in slow circles, drawing out the pleasure, while his fingers spread my lips. His beard tickled my sensitive skin. Without warning, he blew hot breath on my dripping pussy. It almost made me come. When he entered me with a thick finger, I could barely hold it together. He continued flicking his tongue against my clit while two of his hands caressed my thighs. No man had ever done that during sex before. But then, no man I'd ever been with had four hands.

I writhed against him, not caring how loud my moans were becoming. His touch was everything.

By the time he resurfaced from between my thighs, I was teetering at the edge of insanity.

"Please," I moaned, no longer knowing what I was asking for. I just knew that I needed *more*.

Eron chuckled. "Let's see how you like my petals."

He stood up straight, his cock fully erect, his kilt pushed up. I found it strangely erotic that he hadn't taken off his kilt. He was going to fuck me while wearing it. Good. I liked that. His cock was larger than any I'd seen before. The basic shape was similar to that of a human male, but there were rings around the shaft that made me shiver with anticipation. At the top, six flower-like petals hid the head. They glistened with moisture. Pre-cum? Something else? Who cared.

He pushed my legs even further apart, standing between them, his cock in his hand.

"Let me know what this feels like," he said hoarsely and pushed his hardness against my opening. The petals vibrated; not enough to drive me over the edge but enough to make me groan with pleasure.

"Tell me," Eron commanded.

All I could do was moan. But he didn't accept that as an answer. He stepped back, leaving me feeling bereft.

"Tell me what it feels like," he repeated.

I wanted to cry. "You're evil. Come back."

"I asked you a simple question. Answer it and I'll continue."

He was torturing me and from the smirk on his lips, he was very much enjoying it. He stroked his cock, teasing me.

"It felt good," I breathed. "So good."

"That's vague, but I'll accept it for now."

He took a step forward, his petals pushed against me, and then he was inside, entering me with one hard stroke. I screamed, arching my back which only made him reach even deeper. He was so big. He stretched me to the very limit and it hurt, but it was also exactly what I needed. It felt so right to have him fill me like this.

Eron waited until I relaxed down onto the bed. I both loved and hated him for it. I wanted him to fuck me hard, claim me like he meant it, but I also didn't want to tear me apart.

He leaned forward a little, cupping my breasts. They fit perfectly in his hands. As if I was made for him. Just like he was made for me. The thought made shivers run across my skin. We were the perfect match. We were mates.

"Please," I whispered.

And he complied. He pulled out almost entirely, his petals vibrating against my opening, before pushing back in with renewed energy. He set a steady rhythm while his hands kept massaging my breasts. With one arm, he steadied himself before pushing his fingers against my lips. I smiled, remembering how he'd done the same yesterday. I sucked on them, swirling my tongue around his fingertips, imagining that it was his cock. I'd do that soon, but for now, he was exactly where he was supposed to be. Deeply embedded within me. Every time he entered me, his balls slapped against my pussy while the petals vibrated within me.

The sensations were becoming too much. I was hanging on by a thread. I closed my eyes.

"Come for me," Eron whispered.

And I did. I exploded around him, shattering in the biggest orgasm I'd ever experienced. Electricity raced through my body, making my skin tingle and burn. I was floating, not quite in my body. All the while, Eron pounded into me, the petals rubbing against my inner muscles, stimulating them to keep contracting around his cock.

"Do you want me to pull out?" he groaned. "I don't have the strength to control the petals. Not with you."

His words barely made sense, but I knew that I didn't want him to leave. No way.

"Don't," I panted. "Don't stop."

"You don't know what you do to me, leannan. Hold on tight."

His hands wrapped around mine. Was it to steady him or me? It didn't matter. I clung to him as he fucked me hard.

He came with a roar. Pressure built deep within me, a feeling unlike anything I'd ever experienced. Like a massive tampon was inflating inside of me. He stopped moving, freezing in place, while I felt his seed shoot into my core. I was glad they'd given us a contraceptive injection on the Starlight. Back then, I hadn't thought I'd need it, but now, I was grateful.

The pressure against my inner walls didn't subside. It seemed to grow even stronger. A gentle vibration spread from the point where I was stretched the most. The petals. Their trembling almost made me come again. If Eron reached between us to touch my clit, I would shatter all over again.

Suddenly, Eron began to shake. He collapsed on top of me, crushing me with his weight. I could barely breathe, but I was more worried for him. His eyes rolled back and he started to convulse. His expression was surprisingly peaceful. I hoped he wasn't in any pain.

And I really hoped this would be over soon so I could breathe again.

"I love her," he muttered, his words barely audible. "I love June."

He said it over and over again. I lost count. A hundred times, maybe. A thousand. And with every time I heard him speak those words, I fell in love with him a little more. He'd been scared that he'd reveal his biggest secret while having a seizure. Instead, he was telling me what he felt. Despite the agony of seeing him in this state, it was beautiful.

"I love you, too," I whispered. I wasn't sure if he was conscious, if he could hear me. I hoped so.

My vision was starting to darken. I couldn't breathe. My chest hurt. And he was still shaking. With his cock deeply embedded in me. This wasn't how I'd imagined our first time together.

Finally, just when I thought I couldn't stand it any longer, he stopped convulsing. His eyes blinked open, then widened when he realised that he was lying on top of me. He pushed himself off the mattress with a groan.

"Are you hurt?" His voice was no more than a whisper.

"I'm fine, don't worry. How are you? Are you in pain?"

He shook his head. "No. Just tired. Exhausted, actually. Did I... Did I say anything?"

So he couldn't remember. It made me strangely sad. I thought we'd had a moment.

But if he didn't remember, I had to hear him say it while he was conscious.

"I love you," I breathed, not taking my eyes off him.

He didn't hesitate. "I love you too, leannan." He wrapped two of his arms around me and turned us so that I was lying on his chest. His lips found mine for a soft, gentle kiss. I had to stop it way too quickly, still out of breath.

"I'm going to fall asleep," he muttered.

"Then sleep. I'll be here when you wake up."

His eyes fluttered shut and his body relaxed. I smiled down at him before laying my head against his chest. He was so warm and cosy. I closed my eyes and breathed in his scent. His cock was still embedded in me, his petals vibrating ever so softly as if reminding me that they were there. I wasn't sure how long it would last. It wasn't practical and didn't give me much room to move, but I loved the feeling of being bound to him in this way.

I felt myself smiling while I was already halfway in the land of dreams.

14

Eron

My mate stared at the taigeis running around the enclosure. "All of those are yours?"

I laughed. "They're only about a quarter of my herd. Some are in the fields behind the farm. The ones here are just the bulls. I have to keep them separate from the females or I'd drown in taigeis cubs."

"Don't they attack each other? I'd have thought that they're territorial."

I pressed a kiss on her freshly braided hair. She'd let me do it while she'd been drowsing in bed. I'd enjoyed braiding her locks. It had been a long time since I'd last did that to my sister's hair, but my fingers remembered quickly and I managed to get the knots all in the right places. I wished I'd had some pearls, but she was just as beautiful without them.

"Nowhere near as territorial as me."

She looked up at me and grinned. "Yes, I can see that." Her hands moved over her abdomen and my grin disappeared.

"Are you in pain? Did I hurt you?"

I'd stayed embedded in her until we both woke up. Even then, it had taken some work to get my petals to dislodge themselves. I'd cleaned her with my tongue before carrying her into the relief room for a shower. She'd oh-ed and ah-ed when I'd engaged the sonic massage. I'd assumed even a backwater planet like Peritus would have access to basic comforts like that, but apparently not. I had a suspicion that she'd spend a lot of time in the shower.

"No, on the contrary. It feels a bit like you're still in there. It's all warm. I don't know how to describe it."

Her words made me want to bend her over and drive my cock into her depths once more. This time without having a fit. I'd have to be careful with that from now on. I'd not considered how much larger I was and had almost crushed her. She still hadn't told me what I'd said. She just smiled every time I asked and told me that she loved me. It's why I kept asking. I wanted her to say those words again and again.

One of the taigeis males approached the fence and stood on his hind legs.

"Can I pet him?" June asked.

"Yes, that's one of the taigeis I hand-reared. He's tame. Here, give him a treat."

I pulled some pellets from the bag I'd slung over my shoulder. The taigeis bull squeaked in excitement.

"Hold out your hand. Keep it flat. If he exposes his teeth, slowly pull back. I've trained them not to bite, but sometimes they get cheeky. This one's one of the tamest bulls I have, though, so you'll be fine."

And if he tried to bite her, he'd become stew. June may have been opposed to eating my livestock, but she didn't know what they tasted like. I might be able to smuggle some into a soup.

"Aw, he's so cute," she cooed when the taigeis licked the treats off her hand. "Will the cub be as big as him?"

"At least. His father is the largest bull I own, so I expect him to reach the same size or more. Lots of meat to sell."

She glared at me. "I won't let you eat him. Or sell him. I've got a much better idea."

"Aye?"

June grabbed some more treats from my bag. She was going to spoil my animals rotten, I could see that now.

"We should start a petting zoo. People can come and play with the taigeis. You said that most people have never seen one because they're so rare. I'm sure they'd pay to be able to cuddle a taigeis. Children, especially." Her expression fell when she realised what she'd said. "Sorry. I forgot."

I pulled her to my chest. "Even I sometimes forget. But now that you and the other Peritan females are here, we may have Albyan children running around once more. And maybe, one day, one of those children will be ours, leannan."

She wrapped her arms around me, hugging me tightly. "I think I'd like that. And what does that mean? You keep calling me that. Leannan."

"It's hard to translate, which is probably why you didn't learn the word with the BrainTrain. The simplest translation would be sweetheart or my love, but it's so much more than that."

"Leannan," she said. Hearing the word tumble from her lips made me want to kiss her. And so I did. She opened to me, her soft lips ready to be worshipped. She tasted of sweetness and new beginnings. I could have kissed her forever.

My communicator vibrated in my sporran. I groaned. I had better things to do than to answer the call, but June had other plans. She untangled herself from my embrace and stepped back.

"Go, you deal with that and I'll feed the taigeis."

"Treats don't count as food," I grumbled. "See that sack over there? That's their proper food. If you want, you can fill their troughs."

I checked my communicator. Cyle. I sighed before answering the call. "What's up?"

"We'll be with you in ten clicks. Just thought I'd give you some warning in case you continued what I hear you started at the welcoming ceremony."

"He means sex!" Jenny shouted from the background.

"Ten clicks?" I repeated. "That's very soon. How about telling me a bit earlier next time?"

Cyle snorted. "I sent you lots of messages. It's not my fault you never check them."

What an insolent male. Pity he was Albya's First Scientist and therefore highly respected by everyone who hadn't known him as a child. People would be horrified if I told them all the things we used to get up to. Most of the time, Cyle had been the instigator.

I stopped the call and hurried to June. "You better put some clothes on. Cyle and Jenny will arrive here shortly. I'm not sure if Thorrn is also coming."

My mate grinned at me. "You told me to wear this."

"Yes, while we were alone." I hungrily stared at the two strips of clothing barely covering her breasts and arse.

I'd made her outfit from the torn-up parts of yesterday's ugly fabricator clothes. She'd only agreed to wear them after I'd worshipped her pussy into oblivion. I could still taste her.

"I'll make something in the fabricator," June said and handed me the bag of taigeis food. "And do you have any snacks that aren't for animals? I'd like to offer Jenny something when she gets here. Girl chats are always best with snacks."

I didn't know what a girl chat was and I decided I didn't want to know. Back when June had asked to talk to Jenny, she'd been upset. I hoped Thorrn's mate wouldn't cause confusion or make her doubt her decision to stay with me. But no. Jenny had mated an Albyan and now helped Peritan females get settled on our planet. She'd be just who June needed.

I was barely done feeding the taigeis when Cyle's sleek shuttle landed. His was about ten generations more advanced than my own. He hopped out first, then held out a hand to help Jenny. That meant Thorrn wasn't with them. He wouldn't let his brother take over his role as the attentive mate we all aspired to be. I led them into the house where June waited for us. She wore a simple blue dress that hugged her figure, revealing more than it hid. She had a bowl full of manta shells.

"Look, I found this. They look like crisps." She showed them to me and I had to resist breaking into laughter. Unfortunately, Cyle didn't have the same restraint. He cackled loudly. It made me want to rip out his throat.

I took the bowl from her hands before she poisoned herself. There was a particular way of eating manta shells and I wasn't planning on showing it to her today. "I'll get you something better," I promised. "There must be something in the cooler."

Cyle chuckled. "I would be shocked if you have anything but ready-meals and taigeis meat." He turned to June and held out a hand. "I'm Cyle, by the way. Eron is a childhood friend of mine."

"And he's my brother-in-law," Jenny added. "Kind of. They don't have a term for that in Albyan Prime. Cyle hasn't found a mate yet, but he's very interested in the two of you. He's here to run tests and I'm here to make sure he doesn't get too enthusiastic." She shot him a mock glare. "He's been prodding and measuring me ever since I arrived."

"There's a reason for that," Cyle said, suddenly serious. "You Peritans are our only hope of surviving as a species."

Jenny waved him off. "Yes, yes, I know. Do you want to tell them the other news or shall I?"

I grunted. What else did they want? They were keeping me from spending time with my mate. Alone. Without intrusions and interruptions.

Cyle smiled again. "I have been bestowed the right by the Elders to conduct handfasting ceremonies. If you want, I can do yours. Are you waiting...I mean...Are you following traditions and..."

"He wants to know if you've had sex," Jenny snickered. "And if not, he can do the handfasting for you so you can jump into bed."

I exchanged a look with June. Her cheeks had reddened. I decided that I loved when I was the cause of that colour change, but not when it was other people.

"June is my mate," I declared. "She is mine."

The female in question put a hand on my arm and smiled up at me. "What he means to say is that we have no urgency to take the ceremony. It might be nicer to plan it properly rather than right away."

"Exactly," I muttered. "That."

Cyle shrugged. "Pity, I was hoping to see what effect handfasting would have on your hormone levels. We'll just have to conduct those tests later. For now, let's take some base measures. After looking at your DNA, I have some suspicions while the two of you had such an...explosive reaction to each other."

He made us sit on one of the sofas before scanning us with various instruments. All the while, Jenny was chatting incessantly. I wouldn't have been surprised if Thorrn was glad to get some peace and quiet for a few hours, if she was the same while with him. Thorrn was a quiet, grumpy male who rarely said more than what was needed. Jenny was the complete opposite.

"Good, I think I've got the basics," Cyle announced. "Now kiss."

I gaped at him. "You want us to kiss now? In front of you?"

The scientist shrugged. "You didn't have any problem with that at the spaceport."

He should count himself lucky that he was my friend. I would have thrown him into the taigeis pen otherwise.

June, though, was her lovely self as always. She cupped my face and pulled me close until her hot breath mingled with mine. "Let's give them the show of their lives," she whispered before kissing me passionately. For a moment, I wondered whether I should resist - I didn't want to behave like Cyle's lab animal - but I couldn't. Her taste filled my mouth as her tongue playfully bumped against mine. A challenge. I took it. I pulled her onto my lap while kissing her passionately. My chest hurt with all the love I carried for her. This kiss wasn't enough to express what I felt. I ran my hands over her back, caressed her soft skin, played with her braids. My cock was growing hard and I could feel my petals shiver in anticipation.

"Good," Cyle said, pulling me back into reality. "This is very good."

"Pervert," Jenny muttered under her breath. "Get your own mate."

A communicator beeped and I thought it was Cyle's, but it was Jenny who answered it. She used the private call function, so we didn't get to hear who was on the other end of the conversation, but from her short, serious responses, this wasn't good news. June and I broke apart, the moment's magic lost. We all watched Jenny until she ended the call.

"We have to get back," she told Cyle. "One of the women has run away from her match. She sent me a message earlier today saying that she wasn't happy with him, but I didn't think she'd do anything this drastic."

"Who?" June asked, reminding me that of course, she knew all the Peritan females, having travelled with them on the Starlight.

"Beth," Jenny said. "I'll have to go. Cyle, can you do your tests another time?"

The male nodded and packed up his equipment. Even though I hadn't enjoyed being observed while kissing my mate, I had hoped my friend would stay a while longer.

"Do you want me to come with you?" June asked. "I spent a lot of time with Beth. We're friends, I suppose."

Jenny shook her head. "We don't know where she is just now. But once we find her, I'll tell her that you'd be very happy to visit her. Maybe she just missed being around all you girls."

We accompanied Cyle and Jenny to their shuttle. Jenny gave my mate a hug, but I stepped back when she wanted to do the same to me. I didn't want to get in trouble with Thorrn. After all, he was a cage fighter, and it was unwise to get on the receiving end of his fists.

June took my hand as we watched them fly off. "That was a short visit, but I guess it was a good reminder of how special what we have is. The moment I saw you, I knew we were meant to be together. I didn't want to believe it and I still can't quite grasp that I'm going to live on a different planet for the rest of my life, but deep inside, I knew you were mine. It's sad if it's not the same for others. Beth deserves to find her mate."

I wrapped her into my arms. "No mate will ever compare to you, leannan. I'm the luckiest male on Albya. Sgid that, I'm the luckiest male in the galaxy."

EPILOGUE

June

I'd imagined the facility to look like a hospital: bland, sterile and depressing. Instead, I felt welcome the instant we stepped through the front gate. The facility was housed within a medieval castle – had there been any Middle Ages in Albya? – but while the stone walls were old and weathered, inside it was a different matter. Everything was warm and colourful. It felt more like a home than a hospital.

A porter at the gate greeted Eron with a wide smile. "I haven't seen you for a while, Eron. But I can see now why you haven't visited." He held out all four hands to me, looking very proud. "I've heard that Peritans greet this way."

I suppressed a laugh and shook one of his hands. "It's a pleasure to meet you."

"The pleasure is all mine. You're the first awake female I've met in...too long. You give us hope. Thank you for coming all this way."

Eron slipped an arm around my shoulders and pulled me to his side. He still didn't like it when other males got too close. He was getting better at it, no longer growling at them, but we were still a long way off from what I wanted it to be like. Right now, having male friends was an impossibility. Not that I had time for friends other than Jenny. I was too busy working on the farm, developing my petting zoo concept, and spending a lot of time naked with Eron. Especially the latter.

The porter waved goodbye as Eron led me to an elevator disk. We stood on it, Eron's arms protectively around me, and then it rose to the third floor of the castle. Even though Eron had explained that an invisible force field would prevent us from falling off the disk, I was glad he was hugging me.

"I never thought I'd bring a female to visit my sister, let alone my mate," Eron said when we stepped off the disk. His voice was hoarse with emotion.

"You heard what Cyle said. He's getting closer to finding a cure. Soon, you might be able to introduce me to her properly."

He took a deep breath. "Aye, I really hope so. For now, we'll just have to hope that she can somehow hear you."

We walked along the corridor in companiable silence until we got to Dòiche's room. It made me glow with pride that I was able to read the name sign on the door. I still struggled with some of the letters of the Albyan alphabet, but I was improving my reading skills every day. *Dòiche of Clan Monadh.*

Now that we were finally here, I was nervous. Eron's sister was unconscious, yet I still worried if she'd approve of me. My mate talked about her all the time. They'd been close and his love for her was evident in how often he visited her. He'd said that this was the longest he'd ever not come to the facility.

Eron knocked on the door. I shot him a curious look.

"Every time I come here, I like to pretend that she's awake. It's why I knock. It's why I bring her sweets. One day, I hope that I'll open this door and she'll be sitting there, smiling at me."

My eyes burned. Don't cry, June. But he wasn't making it easy. He was the best, kindest, most perfect man in the universe.

I smiled at him and also knocked on the door. Together, we entered a bright, friendly room with the most amazing view across the hilly landscape. The sun was fighting her way through thick clouds and a few rays reached the ground, drenching it in orange light.

Dòiche lay on a hovering bed, a silky blanket revealing her thin body. The wall behind her showed various digital readings and graphs, presumably her vitals. Other than that, there was surprisingly little medical equipment. One of her wrists had a cuff around it which secured a tube that came out of a port in the wall. Maybe that was how she got fed.

Music played in the background, a cheerful jig. I wondered if that had been the kind of music she'd liked to listen to before the Sleep.

"Hey, little sister." Eron sat on the chair by her bedside and pulled me onto his lap. "I've brought a very special visitor. You won't believe this, but I have a mate! Me of all people. Her name is June and-"

"Hi," I said, interrupting him. "I'm June. I'm from a different planet, but I hope that won't stop us from becoming friends."

"Why would it?" Eron muttered. "She'll love you."

I shrugged. "It was the first thing that came to my head."

He stroked my hair, twirling a strand around his fingers. "I know it's strange talking to her like this. Nobody knows if the sleeping females can hear us. But I find it quite therapeutic. Sometimes it helps to say things out loud." He laughed. "I almost hope she can't hear some of the things I told her. If she remembers it all, she'll know most of my deepest secrets."

I reached for his hand and squeezed it. "Just like me. I'm so proud of you for telling me."

For a moment, he froze, then I was in the air, being whirled around until I was somehow facing him. Sometimes, I forgot just how fast he could move. How alien he was.

He looked me straight in the eyes, his expression serious. "It was the hardest thing I ever did in my life. I never thought you could accept me after knowing what I'd done. But I forgot just what an amazing female you are. You're the best thing that could have happened to me. I may not deserve you, but that only means I'll treasure you even more." He moved in for the kill. "I love you, June of Clan Monadh."

I grasped his head and pulled him close, pressing my lips to his. I kissed him, taking control, showing him exactly what I felt about him. He didn't hold back, returning the kiss with a fiery passion, until we were both breathless.

"I love you," I panted, "I love you so much."

He grinned at me, his eyes sparkling with mirth. "Let's find a room. An empty one. With a bed. I have to show a certain female just how much I love her."

I let him carry me in his arms. With my head against his chest, I could hear his heartbeat. I smiled and closed my eyes, listening to that deep sound. He was mine. My mate. And his heart was beating for me.

If you want to know why Beth ran away and if she's going to find her fated mate, read her story in Cyle. Yes, that's a bit of a giveaway. But just pretend that you can't guess who her mate will be.

Get your copy of Cyle:
books2read.com/cyle

Want to know more about how Jenny and Thorrn got together? Read the first book in this series:
books2read.com/thorrn

Would you like your own Albyan Highlander? Join the Hot Tatties Dating Agency:
skyemackinnon.com/hottatties

Want to know what he's hiding under that kilt?
Go to my website to find out!
(*definitely not safe for work*)

skyemackinnon.com/starlightnsfw

ABOUT THE AUTHOR

Skye MacKinnon is a USA Today & International Bestselling Author whose books are filled with strong heroines who don't have to choose.

She embraces her Scottishness with fantastical Scottish settings and a dash of mythology, no matter if she's writing about Celtic gods, aliens, cat shifters, or the streets of Edinburgh.

When she's not typing away at her favourite cafe, Skye loves dried mango, as much exotic tea as she can squeeze into her cupboards, and being covered in pet hair by her tiny demonic cat.

Subscribe to her newsletter:
skyemackinnon.com/newsletter

facebook.com/skyemackinnonauthor
twitter.com/skye_mackinnon
instagram.com/skyemackinnonauthor
bookbub.com/authors/skye-mackinnon
goodreads.com/SkyeMacKinnon